CATACLYSMIC RETURN

TIME'S RUNNING OUT!

Heather Cooper

ISBN: 978-1-961017-59-7 (sc)
ISBN: 978-1-961017-70-2 (e)

Rev. date: 06/22/2023

Chapter 1

The sirens screamed – Loud- deafeningly loud, over every area of the operation station. "The Iron Dome is locked!! It will not close" bellowed Josh Lieberman 'quick, we must change direction of the laser tipped missiles. They are on course to destroy our station, never mind our very existence.

Josh was frantic, fingers flying over the keyboard – changing keys as fast as his mind could think. More by luck than good judgement the missile started to tip over to the left, marginally."Look" Ari shouted, "Its changing course. Oh no! This is causing an even bigger problem as the area off to the left is going to hit Jerusalem, and the TEMPLE MOUNT. Quick, quick, quick, we must get this weapon to change course".

They both knew The Temple Mount in Jerusalem was the most revered Holy spot on the planet.It is revered by the three main religions – Christian, Muslim and Jewish.Now a laser tipped KORNET Russian anti-tank missile was heading straight for Al Aqsa mosque.What more could they do?

"Pray?" said Ari."Never mind praying" said Josh "we must deflect this missile. Like now! Quick, grab the other controls we have to fight fire with fire...

This is a laser beam missile so to change the trajectory we have to use a double beam to knock it off course.Use the T.V.C.If you hit the 'tail and fin' and I hit the main wing we can spin this thing round like a corkscrew and send it crashing into the desert now!Quick, quick, no time to lose"

It was like playing one of their computer games only they were playing for much higher stakes, their very existence!If these missiles hit the temple mount then for sure it would spark World War 3.The devastation and utter destruction simply did not bear thinking about.

The ops room was crowded now, with everyone on the station piled in.There was hardly any sound but you could feel the fear and tension.This was not a game being played for fun or competition.They simply had to find a way to work together to divert the path of the missiles and they had to do so quickly. Josh caught the coordinates, as did Ari seconds later.Now they could change the flight path.It was still tricky and they could not afford any mistakes.Josh's beam caught the tail. Whew!The first missile was turning up, up and up.They had to follow it with steady hands and then Josh shouted "Now".Both radar beams caught the weapon on full power and blasted it away from the towns and cities into the wilderness around Qumran.They had no time to lose; a second missile was coming ever closer."Right same again" said Josh "both beams, same co-ordinates. Now!" shouted Josh "yes, yes its turning its going, yes, yes its gone! Now I can thank God for that, as he turned and gave a short nod, to his colleagues. The missiles had landed out of sight in a very deep gorge in an area around Qumran which is arid, barren and completely inhospitable. There were loud cheers and huge sighs of relief all around the station. That really was too close for comfort.

"Now we can thank your God Ari. That was a close call"

"Brilliant job guys that was a close call" said the station commander, Ben Silverman."We were lucky tonight.The terrorists from Isis, Hamas and Hezbollah won't give up.Their avowed intent is to wipe every Jew off the face of the earth.My biggest fear is that they will get hold of an E.M.P.A seriously powerful electromagnetic pulse much like the one we have developed, they are lethal. Just think! We would be in serious trouble. Israel is a small nation only 260 miles long and 70 miles wide, in fact only 9 miles wide in some places. An electromagnetic pulse used as a missile would wipe out every electrical connection in the country. NoWi-Fi for Internet, no mobile phones, computers, emails, TV, radio, defense, news, no cash from ATM's, no bank, nocredit cards. They would be worthless anyway as there would be nothing to buy. We would run out of food, heating, lighting, petrol.All industry closed down, no fresh water, livestock, no feed for our animals.Our hospitals would not have the power or machinery keeping our friends and family alive. No kid's games even, that means literally, no peace... We have had a salutary warning today and an amazing escape.We can't afford to slip up here guys; we need more drones giving us more warning, much earlier warning.The missiles tonight were fired by Hezbollah probably from Maroun El Ras in Southern Lebanon. We were lucky tonight.They only need to get lucky once.Let's meet in the morning to de brief, work on better solutions.Right now!Rest and a good nights sleep. Well done guys see you in the morning."

Chapter 2

David Lieberman and Joseph Abrams were on their way home from school, a bit later than usual as they had musical recital exams coming up. David was a tall, handsome, sensitive lad, musically gifted, with a funny, quirky, sense of humour, though he tended to be a bit overly serious for his 16 years. His father was Joshua Lieberman head of the ops station at Dimona, and a field director in Mossad, Israel's secret service agency. His mother Ruth taught math and chemistry at the local High school. David had two elder brothers Joel: a bacteriologist, and Gershom, who had recently finished his internship training to become a fully-fledged Doctor in Hadassah Hospital, Jerusalem.

Home for the lads was the small village of Kiryat Arba in the Hebron area of Samaria and Judea if you were Jewish and known to the Arab population as The West bank. There had been serious skirmishes between the Arab and Jewish population for many years, never close to being resolved as both factions considered the land theirs. Peace seemed light years away as nothing looked like being resolved any time soon.

****

The Jewish scriptures record that God made a covenant with Abraham 2000 years before Christ was born. The scriptures also record that God gave the land of Israel to the Jews.Abraham purchased the cave at Mach-pela for 4oo shekels as the burial place for himself, his wife, Sarah, son Isaac (the same son that Abraham almost sacrificed on Temple Mount, still in dispute between Jews and Arabs today.) Also buried at Mach-Pela are Isaac's two wives Leah, and Rebecca, his son Jacob, who fathered 12 sons giving birth to the 12 tribes of Israel. Joseph was buried in Mach-Pela later.

Hebron was King David's capital for 8 years until King David bought the land on Temple Mount for 600 shekels of gold. However it was King David's son King Solomon who built the First Temple in Jerusalem. This stood until the Babylonians destroyed the Jewish temple in 960 B.C. (before Christ.) and took the Jews into captivity for 70 years. King Cyrus released them to come back to Israel and build their second Temple in Jerusalem. 515 BC. This temple stood for 585 years until 70 years after the birth of Christ. It was destroyed by the Romans after a bitter battle when many thousands of Jews and Romans were killed. Israel was renamed Palaestina Tertia a Roman name to eradicate every Jewish link to the land. Jerusalem was named Aelia Capitolina. Jesus however, before he died, warned his disciples the Temple would be destroyed in their lifetime and shared with them the signs that would signal the destruction to come. He warned His followers to flee to the hills and hide when they saw these signs happening. Many, Jewish believers escaped death and destruction at the hands of the Romans and they wrote down and recorded for us what had happened at that time. Many Jews returned to Israel when the Romans left, so there have always been Jews living in Israel.

(This is possibly why Jews today believe their ancestors bought the Title deeds to Hebron and The Temple Mount: therefore, the land is legally theirs. The dispute rages fiercely today, many Arabs and Jews have died and are still dying today over these land disputes. Scripture has recorded these wars for us and warned us there will be more wars in years to come).

****

David and Joseph were not remotely interested in history as they walked home from school this lovely sunny day, they were simply carrying on as teenage lads are prone to do when David stopped and said "what's that?" "What's what? 'I don't hear anything.'""Hush, listen!!" Out of the blue, a black van came screeching to a stop beside them. Three masked men jumped out, pulled sacks over the lad's heads and bundled them both into the back of the vehicle. The boys were taken completely by surprise, no time whatsoever to react or cry out. They were gagged and trussed. The last thing David remembered was a sharp prick in his thigh and sleep very quickly following. He had been drugged!! why?Who were these men and what did they want with him?

Back home Ruth was in the kitchen cooking the evening meal for her brood when Josh arrived home. He hugged Ruth then said "you will never believe what happened in the ops centre today. We had to deal with a couple of dangerous missiles headed straight for us. Gave us quite a scare I can tell you. No one was hurt though, so that was a relief.It was deflected and neutralized pretty efficiently by the team. It's good to get home to you and the kids and catch up with normal things."Ruth turned quickly. "Wait a minute, hold it right there, you did what today? Missiles! That's not all in a normal days work Josh."

"Hey, don't worry!It's what I am trained to do remember.

We are all fine! Honest!How's about a big hug for this hard working guy, who is home now, and starving for some of his amazing woman's home- made cooking..

"Gershom and Joel are still at the hospital so they won't be in until later this evening," said Ruth."David should be in shortly, looking for food, as usual, there is just no filling that boy at the moment."

Chapter 3

The aircraft lurched just as the fasten seat belt sign flashed on. We should be landing in Heathrow shortly thought Gordon. The flight had been uneventful from Oslo to London, where Andrew Balfour and his friend Gordon Anderson had been covering the Middle East peace talks. The talks had not gone well, both the Jews and the Arabs had both walked out (in different directions!!!!) with nothing resolved. The whole scenario was in fact rather depressing, a bit like the British weather typical rain, rain and more rain.

Gordon was a 52 year old civil servant involved with the British Intelligence Service. He was a tall, slender, healthy, fit, distinguished looking gentleman, with blue eyes, and greying hair. Normally he was a humorous, placid, good natured kind of guy, rarely upset by anyone or anything. However at this particular moment, his clean cut features were furrowed in concentration and there seemed to be no trace of his normal good humour. This unassuming thinking man was deep in thought and worried, deeply worried. Gordon nudged Andrew awake and said, "Have you read the Oslo express this morning" "mmm, no not yet," replied Andrew sleepily, pushing his thick blond hair back from his deep blue eyes. Andrew was a handsome young man, with a boyish face, and freckles. At 28 he was young, energetic, and ambitious. He was known to be dogged and persistent, apt to make a nuisance of himself, but these traits ensured he was one of the top political correspondents for UBC better known as the United Broadcasting Corporation. "Why what's worrying you" Gordon handed him the paper which read,

OSLO EXPRESS – 10th September

Colonel Faisal Mohammad, President of Iran still refuses to grant permission to United Nations Peace Keeping Authorities who are requesting freedom to search for suspected hidden weapons of mass destruction. Particularly worrying is the rumour that Hussain has managed to acquire the deadly Matreus Virus.

"Ok" said Andrew slowly. "What is so special about this virus why is this virus more dangerous than any other? They are all pretty nasty. Aren't they?

"Not as much as this one, said Gordon, this is a hot virus!!!!!"

"What on earth is a hot virus? I haven't heard of this one before."

"It's a parasite that cannot live on its own, it duplicates an exact copy of the human body's own host cell, then replicates this rogue copycat cell at lightning speed, the immune system recognizes 'friend rather than foe' and does nothing to fight the silent killer in its midst. With this rapid cell multiplication the natural cells turn to mush and simply explode. It is very similar to the Covid 19 and Aids virus actually. However the Matreus virus replicates at an incredible speed, very much faster than those two, explained Gordon.

"What time scale are we talking about here, how much faster?"

Gordon thought for a moment then said "The Covid virus

tends to hit mostly elderly folks with underlying health issues, with Aids, you will die possibly five to ten years after contracting the virus, but the Matreus virus will kill in only 48- 72 hours' sooner in many cases!"

"What, 48 hours?" repeated Andrew shocked. "You mean only 2 days from start to finish. Good grief that would seem like a nuclear war detonation. This would make the Covid 19 and the AIDS virus for that matter seem no more troublesome than the common cold. How did you find out about this Matreus virus anyway?"

"A very good friend of mine was involved in a hot zone scare last year. Tom Fitzgerald. More commonly known as 'Fitz' He is an American virologist, one of the acknowledged experts in the field. I happened to be in the States at the time and he explained to me why he fears this virus more than any other."

"Do you mean even worse than this corona virus? Most people in Europe America Scandinavia Australia New Zealand Africa Asia cannot conceive of any virus worse than corona. What on earth can be more lethal than that?"' said Andrew. It took a long time for the medics to crack the genetic code of the covid virus and find a vaccine to combat the deadly effects of it. Millions of people died world- wide from that virus, and caused the destruction of most Western economies. People were locked in their homes for months on end, many businesses went to the wall and never reopened so now are you telling me this virus is worse than that?

"I'm afraid it is much worse than that" said Gordon quietly. The serious expression on his chilled features assured Andrew that he was deadly serious. He had never seen Gordon look quite this serious before. He looked haunted. "How on earth can this possibly be worse than corona and how is it transmitted? Is it caught like the common cold, sexually transmitted, or through contaminated needles, blood transfusions? Like flu, tuberculosis, malaria or Ebola?"

"No it is much more lethal than that I'm afraid" said Gordon. "It's an airborne virus which can be breathed into the human pulmonary system and will destroy whole communities of people within a matter of weeks, in fact days in many cases. Anything this virus touches becomes a new host" explained Gordon.

'Uh huh you sure know how to cheer a guy up! If there is any more good news you wish to disclose, now would be a good time to tell me" Replied Andrew.

"As a matter of fact there is, but it has to be kept totally confidential, so I would rather discuss it at my club. I know the information will be kept safely away from listening ears and prying eyes there, surveillance is everywhere nowadays and we can't be too careful with this. I am surprised I am even considering sharing this with you Andrew, but you have contacts and access to places I don't, so I will trust you with this, but, this is important Andrew, you must promise me you will not breathe a word of this to any other person."

"I won't Gordon, you have my word. Sounds intriguing just the same, can't wait to hear what this is all about."

Having managed to secure a taxi fairly quickly, the two men reached the Carlton club and enjoyed a delicious steak meal and a couple of glasses of Tuscany Tignanello. Gordon was now relaxed and ready to share the information lying heavily within him.

Andrew was trying to be patient, but Gordon would not be hurried.

"Let me give you a word of caution Andrew. If what I am going to tell you is true, and I am almost certain it is, then I must warn you this is dangerous information, and if ever disclosed, your life will be in great danger"

"Ok" I get it. I will be careful. What's the betting it will be the best newspaper scoop of my life and I will not be able to print a word of it"

"There is no easy way to say this. MI 5 and MI 6 have both been hacked, as has the American CIA covert branch. In fact I think all of the Secret Service agencies except the Mossad in Israel have been penetrated at the highest level, but as yet we do not know why or by whom."

Andrew was taken aback. It was not often he was rendered speechless but Gordon's grave expression told Andrew this information was not to be taken lightly. Gordon was deadly serious.

"What exactly are you telling me, how can this possibly happen? I would have thought our meticulous elimination process would make this situation impossible. Have you no idea who might be involved or indeed behind this?"

"Nothing concrete as yet, but yes, I do have my suspicions, and a couple of leads I intend to follow up on. This is where your help would be invaluable."

"Bring it on! I can't wait! I have a few favours and some useful contacts I can call on here. Of course I will be careful I know how serious this is"

"Ok, here goes. This is what we know so far. We know there is an international cartel operating illegally, under the radar, this is not a small village operation. It operates world-wide, has vast resources, unlimited wealth and as I mentioned is a global network. We have no idea as to the identity of the brains behind it - they work very much under deep cover on many fronts. I have discovered they have been steadily working in the background for a number of years now" explained Gordon.

"So what alerted you to this particular cartel in the first place?"

"It was Jim Bannerman in Langley who first realized security had been breached. He is based in CIA. We have been close friends for many years, and have worked closely on many operations in some pretty dangerous places. We trust each other. He contacted me last week on my secure line to say that he had intercepted information that had disturbed him greatly. The information so far is that a catastrophic financial tidal wave will roll across all the industrial nations. This cartel are a ruthless shower of individuals, whose one avowed intent is to collapse, and totally destroy, all the major industries, and corporations throughout the industrial worldwhich will mean millions of job losses throughout every nation'

"Good grief Gordon, how on earth has this been happening and no one has noticed until now?"

"Problem with you young folks today, is you haven't studied

history. Let me take you back to the battle of Trafalgar 21st October June 1805.

The battle was between Britain and France, Nelson and Napoleon.

However the background to it all lay in the family wealth of Rothschild. Mayer Rothschild was a German banker who had inherited a great deal of family wealth. He was also a very shrewd banker who had 5 sons so he placed each one of his sons in 5 different European countries. Germany. Britain. France. Italy. Austria. The money was all concentrated in Europe, and between the sons they accumulated more wealth than Croesus. It would be impossible to even guess how wealthy this family would be today. Never mind billions, Andrew. Think trillions.

Nathan Rothschild was based in Britain. He was the financial genius of his day. During the battle of Trafalgar, Nathan had his spies everywhere. They reported that Napoleon was losing the battle. Nathan however spread DIS-information, in fact LIES! The LIES being gossiped around London stated that Napoleon was winning, so the financial sector there sold all their shares, at rock bottom prices. Then with only ten minutes until closing time, Nathan Rothschild bought every single available share on the stock market, and that shot The Bank of England to the very top of the world financial league where it resides until this very day. The Financial centre is in London much to the chagrin of many of our European friends.

The brothers also bought The Central bank in America. Teamed up with Rothschild, Rockefeller, Morgan, lizard, Warburg, Schroder, Schiff.

They first of all created The Council of Foreign Relations in 1921 (controlled by Rockefeller) Bilderberg 1954.

Club of Rome 1968 (also controlled by Rockefeller)

Trilateral commission 1973 (Rockefeller)

However it was the Rothschild's who infiltrated the Free masonic movement and they became a Luciferian society (The Illuminati) 'The enlightened ones' late 1776 approximately.

Today Andrew these people are all working towards a ONE WORLD ORDER a ONE WORLD GOVERNMENT"

"Wait, wait" said Andrew. "I can't get my head around all of this, are you saying, that these secretive people have an agenda, they arecollaborating with other groups all over the world, to set up a one world government?' and it's a group of families primarily? Have I got this right so far?"

"That's fairly close. They work below the radar using 'fronts' mergers and 'buyouts' they back both sides in any skirmish they supply weapons, money, and banking loans. Both world wars are a good example: Britain may well have won the second world war but ended up bankrupt in the process and many financial institutions and families ended up wealthier than they could ever have dreamed of. However the deal is they keep it in family. Family is everything. They are only allowed to marry within family, generally second cousins, nor can they leave the family, if they do, they simply disappear. They are bound for life. Their stated aim, they rule the world, One World Order.

It is becoming easier for them, they use fronts, mergers and buyouts as I mentioned, setting up fictitious companies, with fictitious names where they offer legitimate companies money, vast amounts at that, to sell or merge with them, which in turn allows them to control all the present key industries in all of the different countries. They are buying, bribing, or blackmailing, to get exactly what they have planned. Woe betide anyone who stands in their way, they will simply destroy that individual, and the economy of that country, unless you are one of the main contributing countries, in partnership with them. Now you can understand why it was humanly impossible (almost) for Britain to escape out of the European Union.This is not about money, finance, or the economy. Make no mistake, this is about control. They have unlimited resources, to buy Governments, universities, businesses, companies, commerce, industries, oil, weapons, intelligence agencies,insurance, banks, the press, every news station, television, computers,computer surveillance, CCTV. The best computer operators, who can and do hack into enemy computer systems and that, Andrew, is only part of the problem we are facing today."

"Whew, I get all that, what I can't understand is how they have managed to get away with this for so long without detection?"

"That's the really clever part of this plan" said Gordon. "It has been years and years in the planning for just such a time as this. They have bought and secured the brightest and best minds throughout the world from the world of finance, banking, medicine, law, computers, IT, education, health, Universities. They have head hunted every successful business entrepreneur, male or female. Almost everyone has their price. Not all, but by far the majority can be bought. They groom the top law students, the communication managers, the computer brains. Virtually all of your future leaders have been bought, groomed and trained, ready to be placed in position when the time has been deemed to be right.They have multi-national, international control of all key industries, in all of the industrial nations!"

"This is really scary stuff Gordon, I have never heard of any of this every business, in every city?"

"It would seem so. The very frightening thing about this whole scenario is that they are not financially motivated. This means you cannot simply follow the money as you would normally be able to do. They want power and control, even more than that they want complete control. This is a global strategy comprised of a small circle of dedicated people who are after world domination, they want power and control. Be under no illusion, they are not just wealthy people playing at being wealthy social aristocrats."

"I take it you have given a great deal of thought to all of this, Do you have a plan? Do you have names, places, time scale, specific nationalities, and what do you mean by a global strategy?"

"Hold it, one question at a time, I am explaining as fast as I can.

The strategy is very simple and straightforward. The key is CONTROL.

When you control ECONOMIES, you control GOVERNMENTS.

When you control ENERGY!You control NATIONS.

When you control FOOD!You control PEOPLE."

"Ok, that, I can understand. So what is your strategy, where are we going, and when do we start?"

"First of all we must get on the first available flight that will take us to Israel"

"Israel" Yelped Andrew! totally puzzled at this unexpected answer. "Why on earth do you want to go to Israel?"

"My friend Josh Lieberman is one of the main Field Directors of Mossad, his remit is the Middle East Sector, and as I explained earlier, Mossad has not been infiltrated as yet, certainly not at the highest level. My thinking is, if anyone knows what is going on, you can bet your life Josh will know. I will e mail him now and let him know we will be arriving tomorrow. He will know this is urgent, and will arrange to meet us or at least arrange a company car if he has other business to attend to. Are you Ok with that, or is there any other pressing business you require to deal with before you travel?"

"Not a chance, nothing that can't be placed on the back burner anyway, this is much more important than anything else I had in mind. I can't wait to start."

"Ok. Time for bed and a good night's sleep tomorrow promises to be a long day."

Chapter 4

"Where on earth is David," asked Ruth. "It's just not like him to be this late, especially given all the dangerous upheaval the area has been experiencing lately. Dozens of Palestinian Arabs have been rioting at Joseph's, tomb. They are throwing homemade explosives, firebombs, stones, burning tires, even the little children are throwing stones. I just can't get my head round the futility of this violence, why can't we at least talk?"

"Hmmm" said Josh absently, "even Golda Meir couldn't get Jews and Arabs round the table to talk. Remember she dressed as a peasant girl in dead of night and met up with the King of Jordan to try and stop the war immediately Israel declared independence in 1948. The King of Jordan said he knew Israel would win the war between the Arab nations who would join forces against the new Jewish state, but he could not stand against his Arab brothers as they would turn on Jordan and wipe out his people along with the Jews. The Jews had to win that war, as we have had to win every other war we have fought."

"I didn't know Golda Meir met and talked to the King of Jordan. I knew the history of course, but not all the details. It still doesn't change what is happening today though. We are still at war, and we still have nowhere else to go."

"Ah ha, but some important details have changed. We are no longer a Rag Tag and Bobtail outfit. We have the best weapons in the world today. The AWACs early warning system alerts our analysts instantly any weapon is released, so that the weapon ignites in the country it is released from, way before it ever gets close to our shores. We have the most effective intelligence services, the best operatives we have to as we simply do not get second chances, one effective strike and we are out, but fear not lovely lady, we are the best, so don't worry on that score."

"That is not concerning me greatly at this moment," said Ruth. "My main concern is David. He has never been this late before without giving us prior warning, he knows I worry, especially with the volatile situation at Mach-pela right now. We have our hotheads and our zealous religious crowd as well. I would like to bang all of their heads together and sit them round a table to discuss how we can live together in peace. It's our children that I fear greatly for, I'm feeling really uneasy Josh, I am praying against hope nothing has happened to David."

"Ok just to put your mind at rest, I will pop into the station when I drop Gordon and Andrew at the safe house en route from the airport. I will check the CCTV all the way along the route David and Joseph would take on their way home, see if I can detect where they are. Will that help to ease your mind?You are right though, he would normally phone if he was going to be this late. Give me a call if he comes in while I am driving to the airport."

****

Jordan Border

David Lieberman was still drowsy from the drug that must have been injected into him many hours ago. He knew nothing until he wakened a short time ago in a strange room. He had no idea what day it was, or how long he had been held a prisoner in this place, wherever this place was. The room had white washed walls, with steel bars on two windows, but was clean and comfortable enough with a television in one corner and a book shelf containing books in Arabic!!!! Where on earth am I, and why am I being held a prisoner here, wondered David. I must be in Arab territory, the Islamic time for prayers are being called by the Mullahs from the Minarets.

Suddenly the door opened and a guard admitted a young servant girl, in chador. This isan all - enveloping black mantle garment,with ablack head covering, her face was covered by a veil so that only her eyes could be seen, though she kept her eyes lowered, not even glancing at David. She left a simple meal on a tray for him, and left quickly. David realized he was hungry and tucked into a spicy dish of some sport, the coffee was very strong, but welcome nonetheless. He still had no idea where he was, who was keeping him a prisoner here or why.

****

Ben Gurion Airport

Israel's Ben Gurion Airport was a hive of controlled activity amidst very tight security. "Is all this form filling really necessary" fumed Andrew. "They have gone through everything with a fine toothed comb, at least three times already. How many more forms do we still have to complete?"

"A few more yet" said Gordon. "They are extra cautious these days, far too many people are intent on wiping every Jew off the face of the earth. It will be a while yet I am afraid."

Two hours later, all forms completed, all questions answered, and luggage collected. "At last" said Andrew, "I thought we were going to be stuck there for the duration. Whew, it sure is hot though"

"It is that, however I like the Mediterranean climate, very little rainfall, not like back home where it rains more often than the sun shines"

"That has always puzzled me about Israel" said Andrew. "So little rainfall, yet everything is so green. Everywhere you look something is growing, be it flowers, fruit or vegetables. The Israelis export most of what they grow and are totally self-sufficient in most areas anyway pretty impressive considering."

"Yes they are an industrious, innovative people, they collect as much rainfall as possible and use computer controlled drip irrigation to water their crops and simply recycle the water continuously. It is hard to believe that fifty years ago half of this land was just a mosquito ridden swamp, and the other half a dry barren desert. The Israelis only build, as they still do today on sandy, mountainous areas. It must have taken great feats of engineering to build houses and highways through this kind of terrain"

"What impresses me" replied Andrew "is their superb road

network. It makes travelling around the whole country so easy. Imagine, it only takes four hours to drive from the top of the country in the North to the bottom in the South, and two hours from one side to the other, mind you it is smaller than Wales, only 50 miles wide and 250 miles long. What puzzles me is why all these millions of people are fighting over this tiny piece of land, why can't the Arabs do what the Jews have done and irrigate the thousands of square miles of desert in Arab lands that are totally barren except for a few camels. There are at least 20 odd Arab speaking countries in the Middle East. More if you include Africa, and Asia, they all speak the same language, share the same religion. It would be really easy to use the thousands of miles of barren desert to create a beautiful new homeland for the Palestinians. The Jews can't leave Israel they have nowhere else to go, even now with the rise in anti-Semitism, no country seems safe for them to live in peace. That's always been a puzzle to me, why is everyone out to get them"

Gordon chuckled, "That's a question that brighter minds than mine have struggled with over many centuries. I'm sure it is a great deal more complicated than my simple answer, which would be, politics and religion will forever be a lethal mix. This conflict is all about religion, not a small piece of land"

However their conversation was cut short by someone calling Gordon's name. Andrew turned round to see a ruggedly attractive man, with short receding grey hair, broad shoulders, erect bearing and posture giving away the fact he had a military background. Josh Lieberman walked over to Gordon and shook hands warmly. They chatted for a few minutes, completely at ease with one another, obviously enjoying catching up as old friends do. Gordon introduced Josh and Andrew to one another, and then it was out of the hustle and bustle of a busy International airport, and on their way.

"Would you mind if I just dropped you guys off at the safe house. Fitz arrived on an earlier flight from the States, and is at the safe house already. Your rooms are prepared, it will give you time to eat and freshen up before we get down to serious business. Ruth is worried that our youngest son has not returned home from school yet and is concerned something has happened to him, it's unlike him not to call if he is going to be late. We have CCTV cameras keeping an eye all over that area, as you know it can be a flash point for trouble especially on the Jewish Holy days. It shouldn't take too long to check the route I can then get back and find out what is troubling you. High command has already got wind of something amiss. It will be like old times again with the whole team back together cracking codes."

Chapter 5

Josh walked smartly into the ops room where Ben Silverman was waiting for him. Josh knew instantly it was not good news. Ben looked very serious and greatly troubled. "I'm sorry Josh it's not good. Have a look at the CCTV footage yourself" The CCTV cameras are always operational around the West Bank and Nablus the capital. However it is also disputed territory, the Jews contend that Jacob bought the land centuries ago when he made peace with his twin brother Esau therefore the Jews believe they hold the title deeds to that very revered area. Joshua and Caleb brought their report back to Moses there. Moses commanded the Israelites to make camp and thank God for setting the Jews free from the Egyptians, and allowing them to come back to their ancient land. This area is fiercely disputed territory today. However, Josh Lieberman was not remotely interested in the history of the Jews at that moment in time, he was shocked to his very core to see caught on CCTV the moment his son and his friend were bagged up and kidnapped, thrown into the back of a van, and driven away by three masked men covered in green Hamas battle fatigues. Josh was white with fear and anger. He watched the camera for what seemed like the longest time. Then he spoke, "have we been able to follow them? Do we have any idea where they have gone?"

"We know the direction they have gone, and we know they drove into a warren of a place called Yotvata. Unfortunately we have no coverage there. I think they may have gone close to the

Jordanian border. We will get the lads back Josh, we will have every available person on this case. You know that"

Josh slumped down on the chair closest to him and accepted the cup of coffee handed to him. "I know Ben, what on earth am I going to say to Ruth? This has always been her deepest fear, that one of the lads would be killed or captured, or worse!!!! All of our kids have to sign up for active duty when they are 18 going into all sorts of dangerous situations, it's a miracle more of our kids do not lose their lives. However right now I am only interested in one, my son!"

"We had an emergency meeting of sorts before you got here, and what came to my mind was Elana. We have been married for 40 odd years as you know, but she has been meeting up with this group lately. It's a motley group of Christian Arabs, Messianic Jews, and folks like us more Orthodox in their religion. I think the idea is they are trying to get some cross party dialogue going with the different groups of people to get more understanding and cooperation in our towns and villages. Maybe talk to one another instead of killing one another. Live in peace.Sure they are radical, but they are our best bet for contacts and information. They live there, in among all the hot heads and radicals who are doing their best to cause uprising and war between us. The people who meet up have no love for these agitators who are destroying their lives, or the lives of their children.Elana is coming here as we speak. She has spoken to the leaders of her group. They know who they can trust. If anyone can find out information for us they can. They live among them, so they can go places we can't.Elana has said she would like to go home with you and support Ruth. They have been friends longer than we have, and you will be needed back here. You know what women are like they talk a problem to death we on the other hand, just want to knock the other guy out cold. Oh. Here she is now"

"Josh, I am so very sorry" said Elana, giving Josh a bear hug "we will find David. My friends and I have set up a prayer meeting over 24 hours. We have eyes and ears everywhere. They will not have harmed David, I expect the people who have taken David want to do a trade of some sort. Come, let's go see Ruth. She will know by now something has happened to David. She will be waiting for you to get back to her with some news"

"That is what worries me" replied Josh "how am I going to tell her David has been kidnapped. This has always been one of her worst fears in fact it is every Jewish mothers worst fear living in Hebron"

Chapter 6

David was finding the hours so long and tedious. He saw no one except the young servant girl who brought his food, and clean clothes for him. All his attempts to talk to her or the guard were totally ignored. He knew the girl understood him, living in the West bank area he was bi lingual and spoke Arabic pretty well. As the young Arab girl came in with yet another tray David tried again. "Please, don't run, can you at least tell me your name? You know I will not harm you." At last the young girl glanced at him, only for a second. She whispered "Meara" Then ran out of the room. David knew she would not have spoken to many strange men, other than close family members. Most Arab women live in seclusion behind the veil, in women's quarters, separated from the men, so he knew he would have to tread slowly and very carefully, very gently, with this young lady.

Over the next couple of days, David purposely left his room messy so that Meara would have to stay longer to clean up. Then David totally confused her by helping her to clean up!! This is unheard of in Arab culture as men would never do anything that would be deemed or seen as women's work. Meara had never encountered a situation like this before. David's patience, however, paid off and she started to relax and even became quite chatty with him. He made outrageous, humorous comment's that made her laugh. Eventually she began to trust him. He asked her where they were and she told him, "Yotvata, near the Jordanian border" "Do you know where they have taken my friend Joseph? He was taken captive at the same time as me? "No I haven't heard of anyone else being held a prisoner anywhere, but I will ask my friends if they know of any other young lads being held prisoner like you are here" David asked her if she ever went to the market, with any of the other servants, but Meara said no, she very seldom left the house. David realized he could not pass a message out that way. However he wasn't about to stay locked up in this room for the rest of his life either, somehow he was going to escape. He chatted to Meara and told her what life was like outside the compound, a world she could scarcely comprehend, but a plan was forming in David's mind. The problem was, he would require Meara's help to execute it. Meara would have to come with him she couldn't stay here, as her life would be in danger if she did not escape with him.

One morning David said "Have you ever considered what life must be like outside these four walls Meara?""Of course" said Meara in surprise. "I know the world outside of here is a huge amazing interesting place. I read my brothers books. I bribed my brother to teach me to read when were younger. I know life is very different for girls in other countries. What is it like for Jewish girls in your country?"

"Very different from your life here the girls and women are very equal with the men in our country, they even have to do two years military service the same as the guys. I wouldn't argue with one of them for sure. They are tough. They have careers of their own in every industry, go to University, come out as Doctors, nurses, medics, lawyers, teachers, own their own businesses, chemists, pharmacists computer programmers, research scientists. Golda Meir, was a much loved Prime Minister in Israel, so our women can do anything and go anywhere in the world. They have careers, earn their own money, buy their own flats very liberal are our women.

"But what about marriage and having babies asked Meara in astonishment?"

"Oh, they do that too! Very much on their own terms though, they would not stand for arranged marriages or anything like that.

"This I cannot imagine" commented Meara wistfully.

"Would you like to see the world Meara?"

"Oh yes! David. Very much, but I will never be able to do that. I would be too frightened, I am not educated. I would have nowhere to live."

"You could come with me. I promise I would look after you, my mum has always wanted a daughter she would just love you as she must feel a bit outnumbered living in a house with four men.

"What are you saying David. How can this be? We are both prisoners in this house we can't just walk out the door guards would shoot both of us without a second's hesitation!"

"I know we can't walk out the front door, but you can bring me some women's clothing. You don't know who on earth is under that big black kaftan covering, I can cover myself with a Burka. You call Yousefin for something and I will be lying in wait to knock him out cold - that would give me great satisfaction! We walk quickly to the women's quarters, hide until dark, then we escape. We can do this Meara, what do you think?" David saw great fear in Meara's eyes, but also something else, a great desire to leave the compound and experience a life she knew would be possible away from the confines of her life here. "I have Muslim friends where I live" said David. I would introduce you, so it wouldn't be completely new to you, but it would be your life Meara, there is so much for you to see and do and become. The world would be your oyster"

"David, I am not a Muslim" said Meara quietly.

Now that rendered David speechless, for a moment anyway a most unusual occurrence.

"But I thought all Arabs were Muslims!"

"The majority are, but not all. My grandmother went to the missionary school and they taught us all about Jesus. They taught her how to read and write so she read to me when I was young. She taught me how Jesus was a Jew, from Israel, just like you. Surely you know all about Jesus?"

"I have heard of him sure, but we are not encouraged to talk about Him"

"We can't talk about Him either. If anyone leaves the faith of Islam, at the very least they would be banished, many simply disappear"

"You mean murdered?"

"Well I don't know if that is the case, but they disappear anyway. There are some of us who are Christian, two of the older ladies go to a secret meeting of Christians, Amah would help us, she already knows all about you."

Chapter 7

Ruth was exhausted after many hours of tears, recriminations, discussion, ideas, going round and round in circles eventually accepting a sedative to help her sleep. Elana stayed overnight with her and suggested she stay to give support for as long as necessary, at least until David and Joseph were both found and brought safely back home again. Josh had returned to the Ops centre where the cobra team had arranged a meeting to plan the strategy that would find the two lads.

****

Operations Planning Room

In another section of the Underground Military Command Centre, a very important meeting was taking place between Mordecai, one of the senior Mossad departmental heads, and Tom Fitzgerald who was an American bacteriologist, along with Gordon and Andrew. Top of the agenda was the Matreus virus. Where was it being stored, and how a Mossad operations team could acquire some samples of the virus to enable the scientists discover an antidote or vaccine to combat this deadly virus. A virus created in a lab is in fact a bio terrorist weapon, created by human scientists so they create the Genetic code. And thereby hangs the problem: It is virtually impossible to discover a Vaccine if the genetic code is with-held for any reason. Mossad had been compiling a dossier for almost 2 years with a deep cover intelligence team operating in Syria all along the Golan

Heights and deep into Syrian territory. Mossad knew that ISIS terrorists had stockpiles of this deadly virus stored somewhere. They were using the latest scanners to alert the operatives if they came into contact with the organism. It truly was a deadly organism with no known antidote. If ISIS filled a warhead with this virus and unleashed it into Israel, millions would die. They had to find this stockpile. The Mossad team was led by Yacov Meier, a big, good looking, fit, healthy, dark complexioned Jew who could easily pass for an Arab, and spoke several languages fluently. Along with Simeon Weissman who was slighter in build, also very dark complexioned, with a mop of dark curly hair, dark brown laughing eyes, even white teeth, and a wide smile. He often laughed and smiled easily, but not tonight, the conversation was deadly serious. They had received instructions from headquarters it was time to go into the underground tunnels and steal some samples of this deadly virus. They needed the genetic code to produce the vaccine that would save literally millions of lives. Both Mossad operatives were good friends with the Kurds who had also lived on the land for many generations. Their forbears were descended from the Elam tribe of Jeremiahs time. They had been almost wiped out but not completely.Scripture records they would rise again as a nation to be reckoned with in the latter days before The Messiah returns. They had been observing a great deal of suspicious coming and going of military personnel, noted top level Russian scientists, movement of arms, warheads, and rockets. This very selective secretive team had been conducting top secret scientific studies in some concealed underground tunnels. These tunnels were very deep, well lit, closely guarded, had rail tracks running for miles underground. However, Mossad were the best undercover operatives in the business. They had to be! They were also well prepared, and had done their homework well, with compiled maps, details, passageways. The team had hit a snag when they came up against reinforced steel doors, well and truly locked. Something very sinister was hidden behind these steel doors and the team intended to find out exactly what was hidden behind these doors. The Kurds were able to pass for natives so some of them along with the two Mossad agents had infiltrated the ranks of ISIS and able to shout 'Alahu Akbar' (God is greater) with the best of them. They had become trusted members of the ISIS team, so no one took a great deal of notice what they were up to.

"Ok" said Yacov, "tonight's the night. We have been given instructions to steal some samples of that very nasty stuff they have concealed behind those hidden, reinforced doors. We will have to pretend we are all coming out after our shift, but stay behind, hidden until all is quiet, then we go after the stuff and simply disappear, back over the border when we get the containers" They would wear special fatigues which are wonderful for concealing all sorts of weapons, electronic listening devices,deactivators for destroying alarms quietly, tiny magnetized lock prongs, small intensely high powered pen lights with blue beams, special electronic stethoscope listening devices, climbers ropes wrapped around their waists, immobilizing canisters of gas, taser guns, explosive discs. They were as prepared as it was possible to be, they were both excellent cooperatives, superbly well trained, good at their jobs, the best in the business they had to be simply to stay alive. Yacov explained their plan of action one more time, until everyone knew exactly what was required of them, so now all they could do was wait until it was time to move.

****

SAFE HOUSE

David was so excited when Meara decided after much deliberation that she wanted to escape with him. She had confided that she was going to be married soon as the master's fourth wife. This prospect did not appeal to her at all so being offered this chance to escape and do something different with her life appealed greatly. Meara decided she was up for the challenge: she wanted to escape with David.

"Fourth wife" remarked David. "Good grief must tell my dad that one he has enough bother coping with one!!! Do you think Amah would help us to escape?"

"I'm not sure," said Meara, "but I know I can trust her. She knows I am unhappy here, and I definitely do not want to get married. I do not want to be stuck in a house with nothing more to look forward to than having sons, cooking cleaning and keeping house. I want to learn to do other things, learn about the world, study, and travel, meet someone of my own choice and then get married and have sons. Daughters also, but they would be free. I can't even go to the market, and never ever by myself"

"Wow that was quite a serious statement. Are you absolutely sure you want to come with me?"

"Yes, I'm sure. I have given much thought to this. I will speak to Amah tonight, ask her what she thinks. She will know best how to escape from the compound. I had better go now though, as Yousef will be getting suspicious"

David spent a restless night waiting for Meara to come with his breakfast the next morning. "Well did you speak to her?"

"Yes I did. She said she will help us escape, but we must be patient until we have a good plan in place. Then we will need somewhere to hide, I cannot get caught trying to escape, things would not go well for me. Amah is going to talk to some Christian friends tonight"

"More waiting" said David, falling back on the bed in frustration. "I am going to go crazy looking at these four walls for one more day"

"Better crazy than dead I think" said Meara. "I want to see the world, not die before I have lived!"

"Ok, guess I will have to be patient for a few more days"

****

Golan Tunnels

Everyone else had left the tunnels and gone above ground for a good hot meal, comfortable bed and sleep. It was eerily quiet and freezing cold. They too were hungry, at least they had some bottled water, and some bread and cheese. It wasn't much but it would have to suffice meantime.

"Ok time to move" said Yacov. "It will help the circulation a bit, and warm us up if we move now. Everyone should be well above ground and eating a lovely home-made hot meal at this time. It should be safe enough to move and get through the steel doors let's go" They reached the doors in record quick time. Managed to disable the alarm, using some of their fancy electronic prongs equipment, opened the door easily enough, and they were in. It was very dark, and very smelly, a very powerful pungent sulfuric disgusting smell. "Oh man, something smells, very dangerous to my health right now" said Simeon, "best put mask on I think!" As they walked carefully along a stone pathway, Yacov kicked away some rubble, and one of the stones landed with a thud."Did you hear that Simeon?" "No -hear what?" "That block over there, it gave off a different sound, a kind of hollow sound" "Have you got the crowbar handy? I want to investigate the different noise, help me clear away the rubble then I can use the spade to lift that block over to the left.

'It is heavy, but moving slightly. I guess the exercise should heat us up a bit stop us complaining, build strong muscles....."

'Ok it's moving, it's going, slide it along, look it's a deep hole."

"Yes I can see that" Commented Simeon cautiously, "I suppose you are going to say we go down and have a look. Think I would rather go home now. Thank you"

"Well you can't. We are too close to back off now. Toss up for the pleasure of going down the hole first!"

"Damn!" said Simeon, as he lost the toss. "Just make sure you hold on very tightly to that rope!"

Movingvery slowly, Simeon reached a ledge. Calling quietly to Yacov "Anchor the rope securely and come on down, this must lead somewhere" Simeon shone his torch and watched as the rats scuttled in every direction. The tunnel was pitch black, pungent smelling and as slippery as an ice rink. "Careful Yacov, move slowly here, this ledge is getting narrower and narrower. It looks a long drop down there"

"Yep, I had noticed! Just be careful you don't slip or we both go down. I wonder where this leads to?"

"ssh! Listen, can you hear something?" "Yes, sounds like a whirring noise over to the left. I think I see a light" "Ok I see it" Moving stealthily, very carefully, they crawled closer to the light. Then Simeon stopped raising a hand in warning. "I can see a guard, over to the left. He is lighting something, a cigarette probably"

"There is another one that makes at least two. Wonder how many more guards are down here? At least we know we are in the right place, they must be protecting something"

"We will have to take them out sharpish, we don't know how many of them there are down here"

"Ok, let's get this done as quickly as possible" Without making a sound, the two Mossad agents crept slowly behind the two guards. With cold ruthless efficiency, Simeon heard the guard's neck 'snap' as it broke. Yacov disposed of the other guard with equal efficiency.

"Have you got the prongs? Let's get this door open"

"Wow, would you look at this? A real Alladin's cave" said Simeon. They found themselves in the largest military base they had ever seen. It had been tunneled out through earth and rock, and reinforced with special steel. There were missiles, canons, rockets, surface to air missiles, armoured vehicles, a special radar and electronic communications system, and sealed canisters, containing something guaranteed to destroy good health.

At that very moment an ear shattering alarm bell resonated throughout the entire area, and with it being underground, the sound echoed to a deafening roar.

"Run!" Shouted Simeon "Where to smarty pants?" whispered Yacov.

"Back the way we came" but they were too late.

Chapter 8

"Davidlisten" said Meara excitedly. "Amah spoke to her Christian leader last night. He said it is a bad thing that Faisal has kidnapped you,keeping you locked up here, so he will help us to escape. It's all prepared for tonight"

"Tonight!!!! I didn't expect the answer to come back so quickly" Brilliant! let's get this done. I am desperate to get out of here, and back home to my parents.They will be so worried about me, ok what do we do?"

"Can you ride a motor bike?"

"Yes of course, I have been on my brothers lots of times, though Mum wouldn't let me have one of my own"

"That's great. I will bring your evening meal as usual, however I will have on two sets of clothing. I will call Yousef into the room, you will be ready to knock him out cold and tie him up. We can put him onto the bed and cover him up as if it is you in the bed. Do not kill him he is just following Faisal's orders. We then lock the door and escape through the women's quarters. They will not expect that as no self- respecting Arab male would ever wear women's clothes. Amah will be waiting for us and she will let us out. She has given me a map for you to study so that we will know where to find the Christian leaders house. We must stay there for a while until we can smuggle you back to Israel.

'Fantastic!" said David. "I can't wait for tonight. Yes!!! home soon. We will get away, I just know we will!" Every minute seemed like an hour as David waited for Meara to come with his evening meal. At last she arrived, and quickly stripped her outer chador for David to put on. She giggled nervously at the picture he presented, but it was a good disguise.

David stood behind the door as Meara called on Yousef. The young Arab did not know what hit him as David knocked him senseless. "Quick! Tie him up very tightly, put him on the bed, cover him and let's get out of here" Meara picked up the tray and went out the door. The way was clear so she motioned for David to follow her. They walked quickly to the female quarter where Amah was waiting for them. Amah hugged Meara tightly to her then motioned for them both to follow her. They were almost at the gate when a guard shouted for them to stop. Amah screamed and ran at the guard who opened fire and shot her. Meara was turning to go back to her when David grabbed her hand, and ran. They ran to where the motor bike was hidden. David jumped on, fired on the ignition quickly, hauled Meara on behind him, and they were off. David was praying fervently to the God he didn't believe in, that the bike would ride, the engine would not cut out, they managed to clear the compound quickly, but very soon the guards were on their tail, many of them. David tried very hard to coax the bike to go faster, but a small bike with a small motor is no match for a powerful car. They were gaining so David had to think and think quickly.

Chapter 9

Deep Inside Golan Tunnels

A guard came running and saw the two men. Yacov glanced at Simeon who understood perfectly. Yacov ran to the left and Simeon to the right. The guard hesitated for a fraction of a second at this totally unexpected move unsure where to shoot first. It was all the time Yacov needed, he pounced on the guard smashing his skull on to the floor with such force blood spewed everywhere. Another guard was following hard on his heels, shouting loudly to alert other guards nearby, his luck ran out as Simeon dispatched him in double quick time with a lethal blow to the nape of his neck. The two Mossad agents reached another door and wrenched it open, unfortunately another guard was waiting and fired, he caught Yacov on the top of his thigh. He could feel the warm blood oozing down his leg. Simeon fired at the same time taking this guard out. More and more guards were streaming down into this small space. There was no place to hide except a large piece of machinery Simeon managed to dive behind.Yacov couldn't run so he was trapped. Simeon heard the Arabs shouting and swearing at Yacov, then beating and kicking him when he refused to speak or answer their questions. Simeon was sweating, thinking furiously. What weapons did he have in his small armoury, it wouldn't be long before they would shoot Yacov if he wouldn't give up the information they wanted to know. He felt for a canister of immobilizing gas, found it, a spray of this would shut them up for a while. He placed his gas mask on, as he released one of the canisters. The guards went down very quickly. Simeon raced to get Yacov's mask on. He was in a real mess the guards had given him a very sound beating. Blood was everywhere, his face was splattered in blood, his right eye was already swollen and partially closed but he would mend, eventually, if they ever got out of this tomb alive that is.

Simeon worked at a furious pace, found the sealed containers he was looking for, and placed them beside Yacov. Now he was going to blow this place sky high. Simeon was angry when he thought of all the millions of lives that would be lost if these weapons of mass destruction were ever used, mostly Israeli lives, but once this virus was loosed then nothing would be able to stop it, unless some of their genius physicians could find the genetic code to render the killer virus null and void. It was no secret that many Arabs and Emirs in many countries wished every Jew dead and cast into the deepest sea. Israel totally annihilated forever, but as Hitler and many other nations like Iraq, Iran, Hamas terrorists in Gaza and Hezbollah in Lebanon have tried, the Jews are not so easily wiped out. They are clever, they have to be, and whether they believe in Him or not they have a mighty God who makes Covenant. It cannot be broken, and THIS God. The ONE TRUE GOD wins every battle HE engages in. However Simeon was not giving a great deal of thought to any religion, Muslim, Christion or Jew, right now, he just wanted to find a way out of this maze of tunnels he found himself in, faster rather than later. This was about to get real messy. However, Simeon also knew if caught in a jam then attack is the best form of defense and he decided none of the weapons in this vicinity would ever be used against his people.

He wired all the explosive discs to the most dangerous looking weapons, with a five inch square globule of semtex explosive a pale clay coloured malleable substance that Simeon packed carefully around the discs. When set alight this would burn through an inch of steel. He set the timers, and prayed he could get himself and Yacov out of the tunnels in time before the whole enchilada blew. The time was set for thirty minutes after the tunnels opened in the morning. That should give them time to be well away from this place and on their way home to Israel.

Simeon pulled Yacov out into the cave, and tucked the sealed canisters in his rucksack. Yacov moaned with pain, but it couldn't be helped. The journey back along the cave was painfully slow, but at least there were no more guards around.

At last Yacov woke up, and this time really yelped with pain. "Ah my arm, it must be broken. My leg is injured, I don't know if it will take my weight. I sure am sore all over!"

Simeon scrabbled in his medical kit and found a couple of temgesic tablets "Here, have a couple of these, they should help a bit. Can't give you anything stronger I need you to try and walk a bit. Lean on me we have to get out of here. Can you walk?"

"I don't know. I hurt in places I didn't know existed. Help me up. Ouch, they must have broken a couple of my ribs, kicking me with their big heavy tack boots, not the friendliest of natives I have encountered on my travels"

"Well nothing is surer than we will be history if we don't get out of here before morning. This place is going to go up in smoke with the biggest almighty bang you ever heard in your life, and if we are still stuck down here then we go up with it. We will not be like humpty dumpty and all the tiny bits put back together again. We have to get out of here now. Lean on me. We can do this!"

Chapter 10

David was driving as fast as he dared, ducking and diving down alleyways that would be difficult for a car to follow. He had pored over the map, memorized every turn and committed the map to memory. Fortunately he had excellent recall, and an almost photographic memory. Young boys start reading and memorizing the Torah at 2 years of age. This exercise gives them a great head start over other children in other nations, and allows many Jews to excel in various strands of academia for example, chemistry science medicine arts, inventions and innovations.Whoever had compiled this map had taken into account the young couple might be pursued, so he had them take a roundabout route, easy for a motor cycle, very difficult for a car to follow. They lost the tail, and they were free. David was overjoyed, Meara less so. Then it dawned on David, Meara's friend had probably died helping them to escape.

David was quiet then reached out to Meara. '"I am so sorry Meara I know how much Amah meant to you" Meara allowed him to comfort her, for a short time as she cried for her friend. However Meara knew they had to find Amah's friend's place soon, they were not safe yet. "Faisal's men will be in deep trouble if they go back without us"

"Now that will not trouble me in the slightest" said David.

Slowly and carefully, they made their way to the address David had memorized first making sure no one had followed them. The door was opened by an elderly gentleman who said, 'shukran' welcome, and bade them enter. The room was dark, lit only by a small lamp, but it was warm and very safe. Both Meara and David felt that instinctively. The elderly gentleman introduced himself as Pastor Hussein. There was a calm, gentleness about him that allowed David and Meara to relax. Pastor Hussein had beds made up, one on the floor for David, and another bed made up in the room for Meara. After a light meal, he suggested they sleep, saying there would be plenty of time to talk in the morning.

David awoke the following morning to the most delicious smell of breakfast cooking, eggs and pancakes. "Where on earth am?" He had many questions, but they wouldn't be answered lying in bed. It was time to get up and have a chat with Pastor Hussein.

"Well good morning young man, are you hungry?" Silly question, what young man of your age is not hungry at all times. Have your breakfast then you can tell me what happened" David shared all the information he had, which was very little. He had no idea why he had been kidnapped, or by whom.

"I think a fairly safe guess would be Hamas would like an exchange to take place, between one or more of their members who have been caught and imprisoned, and in return release your friend and yourself home unharmed. They will not have expected you to be able to plan an escape and persuade one of our Arab girls to aid and abet their prisoner to escape and elude them. Question is what do we do with you both? Your parents will be worrying therefore we must get a message to them to let them know you are safe. My son is a businessman who often travels to Israel on business, and we have many Christian friends there. One way or another we will find a solution to this problem. Yes my young friend you will have to be patient for a little longer and remain as my house guest until it is safe for you to return home. Meantime you are 'my family' come to visit, should anyone ask?"

"We appreciate your kindness em...Mr Hussein?" Pastor Hussein chuckled as he realized this was the first time David had encountered a Christian minister.

"We are not unlike your Jewish Rabbi's David, our heritage is the same. We will have time to have some interesting chats since you will be spending quite some time with us"

"I was kind of hoping I could go home soon" said David wistfully. He felt the pain of missing his family and friends keenly. He knew how much his parents and brothers would be missing him. They did not know he was unharmed and would be coming home soon.

Pastor Hussein was a wise man who well understood how David was feeling. His first priority, however, was keeping David safe. "I think it would be safer if Meara went to Israel with my son Amir, and contacted your brother at the hospital. We have western clothes for her. No one has seen her without her veil, so she would not be recognized. How would you feel about that Meara? "Yes, I would rather do that than get married" said Meara vehemently. "The clothes will seem strange at first, but I will get used to them."

"Good, that's settled then. Now, if you will excuse me, our House group meets here this evening, and I have to prepare my talk. We can chat some more later. Come Meara. Selima has laid out some new clothes for you.Hopefully they will fit"

David was not prepared for the shock of seeing Meara in a pair of denims, blue summer top and trainers when she came back into the room some 30 minutes later. He was astonished, but quickly said, "Wow! You look great Meara, you really do! No one will ever recognize you in these clothes. What a brilliant disguise. Wonder if I would look half as good dressed as an Arab? Ok maybe not! Wish I could see Gershom's face when he sees you turning up on his doorstep. I just wish I was coming with you. I miss my mum and dad, and my brothers, my friends, even school"

"I know, but it won't be long before you can leave here and go home, at least you are safe here, and not being held a prisoner any more, they are nice people. I like Pastor Hussein and Selima his wife, they are lovely, I feel very welcome here not a stranger at all. Tell me though what is it like in Israel, what are your parents and brothers like? I don't know what to expect, though I know your life in Israel is very different from my life here"

David spent the next few hours preparing Meara for the very different changes in culture she would experience between her own Arab and Western backgrounds. However, he was totally unprepared for the culture shock he would experience as he listened to Pastor Hussein speaking to the group gathered in his home that evening.

Pastor Hussein welcomed all of the folks to his home. They had time for tea coffee and biscuits, people hugged each other, and enjoyed catching up with close friends. David observed this group of Jews, Arabs and Christians all chatting around like one big family. Then Pastor Hussein called them together to start the meeting. "My subject tonight" said Pastor Hussein, is "Be prepared! Yeshua Ha Machiach is returning soon for His people! Yes David, Jesus our Messiah is returning soon for His people!"

That was David's first shock of the evening, more was to follow.

Pastor Hussein then unfolded a chart that listed all the Old Testament references to the Messiah and cross referenced them with the New Testament scriptures. Anyone could see at a glance that Jesus fulfilled every reference in exact detail. David was astonished as he studied this chart very carefully.

"Then of course there is the time element. Before Jesus was crucified, He sat and shared with His disciples, that He must die to take away the sin of the world but do not fear, HE told His disciples, The Father will give you another Comforter, The Holy Spirit. He will live within you He will comfort you, and never leave you. The things that you have seen ME do you will do also. All Authority and power will be given to you, over all the works of the enemy. Jesus also told His disciples that the temple would be destroyed, not one stone will be left standing on top of the other. History and scripture tells us that both the temple and Jerusalem were both reduced to rubble in 70 AD. Less than 40 years after Jesus death. There are no official temple records after this time, they all went up in flames along with the temple, everything in the temple and surrounding areas was reduced to ashes, so no Messiah within the last two thousand years could trace their direct lineage to the throne of David, as Jesus clearly did, on both His mother and His father's side."

The meeting finished with a general discussion. David observed these Christians very carefully. They enjoyed a closeness with each other, like a family almost. They prayed to their God about everything, as if they knew Him personally and more to the point HE knew them, and they had such assurance that He would answer their prayers. David found all of this extremely confusing to say the least.

Pastor Hussein gave David a cup of coffee, and asked him if he was familiar with the scriptures.

"Well I have listened to our Rabbi teach from The Torah and the Scriptures since I was little boy, but I did not know that Christian's taught from our Scriptures."

"Yes, both Old and New Testaments were written by Jews, except two books, The Gospel of Luke, and The book of Acts, they were written by Doctor Luke, a Greek Physician. Do you not know you are one of the chosen Generation David?"

"Chosen generation? Chosen for what?"

"Yours is the generation that will see the return of Your Messiah"

"What do you mean the return of our Messiah, I thought we were still waiting for him to come the first time around" stated David.

"Why don't you have a chat with Michael, he is Jewish, like

yourself. Mike come and chat to David here, he has lots of questions he would like answers to."

"Sure thing David nice to meet you, how are you?"

"I'm good, just a little puzzled. Pastor said you were Jewish, are you?"

"Yes I am" said Michael with a grin.

"Yet you are obviously one of this Christian group.I just don't get this at all' said David. "How can you be Jewish and believe in Jesus"

'It's not so very difficult I am simply a Jew who firmly believes YESHUA is our Messiah, as well as the Christian Messiah. They call us Messianic Jews. There are thousands of us, hundreds of congregations in Israel alone, especially since Rabbi KADURI died and went to Glory.'

'Rabbi KADURI I know of him, said David. Many of our Rabbi's and folks from our congregation went to his funeral last year.

'They will have done' said Michael. He was very well known and a well- respected Rabbi throughout the world. He was 108 when he died and known as the most devout Jew in Israel in fact the whole world. However what many Jews did not know is he left a codicil in his will. The codicil stated nothing must be opened or read until a year had passed after his death. His son followed his wishes and the note was read out after a year had passed. The contents of the codicil sent shock waves throughout all of Israel. It was written he had seen and spoken with our Messiah. The name written down was, YESHUA Ha MACHIACH, HE is our Messiah.' Yes David, Jesus is our Messiah.

'No way, said young David vehemently, I can't accept that.'

'Don't take my word for it' said Michael. 'Read it for yourself. I have his book here with a photograph of the note in it. There is also a fascinating video you can watch. Then you can make up your own mind as to the truth of what Rabbi KADURI shared. He shared this truth with many of his young Rabbi's in seminary. Don't look so panic stricken young David. This is great news. YESHUA is returning to Jerusalem soon. More and more Jews worldwide are accepting Jesus as our Messiah, because most of the prophesies that point to his return have been fulfilled, especially in the last few years'

'What prophecies' asked David, very interested, despite his better judgement.

'Well, our prophets like Isaiah, Daniel, Jeremiah, Ezekiel all say quite clearly that God warned our ancestors not to worship other false god's. Our people foolishly ignored the Living God, so our scriptures tell us our people were scattered from our land of Israel to the four corners of the earth. However that wasn't the end of the Prophecy. God isn't finished with our people yet. He sent our Messiah exactly as our scriptures foretold. He came to His own but His own received Him not. Jesus told His disciples all these things before He died. Then he said take the good news to all the gentile nations. Israel will be trampled on by gentiles until the TIME OF THE GENTILES END. Jerusalem was back under Jewish control after the six day war in 1967. The times of the Gentiles have ended and Jerusalem is once again the capital of Israel. Now we enter a new age, a new period just before Jesus returns. Whatever way you look at this, God must have helped the Jews to become a nation once again, living in the land of Israel, because in every war, our small nation has had to overcome impossible odds. How can a small nation like ours of only six million people, possibly take on the might of the Arab nations, supported by Russian weapons, and win decisively. Look at the advantages the Arab nations seemingly have. Two thirds of the world oil supply, and a much larger population than ours. Yet all the Arab nations lined up against us could not wipe us out, that just has to be because of our God.

Now get this David. Jesus said. Jerusalem would be free from Gentile domination and back in Jewish hands. God would then bring His people back to the land He gave them, from all the four corners of the earth, and the generation that saw this happen, would see His return. Jesus is coming back for His own, and all the signs point to us being the generation that will be on the earth when Jesus returns, that means you and me David. What a time for us to be living in, it's so exciting.'

"Well" said David slowly, "I sure don't find all this quite as exciting as you obviously do. What happens to all the people who don't accept Jesus as their Messiah?"

"That is the whole point of all this: we have been entrusted with the Good News to warn the people, Jesus is coming back soon with His people, not to die this time on our behalf, but to rule and reign over all the nations' said Michael excitedly"

'Hold it, wait a minute' said David. 'Slow down! I've never heard of any of this stuff before, what do you mean coming back with His people, who are they? Do they come from Heaven with Him? Where is He coming back to and where do you get all this stuff, this information from? And what's more how do you know all this is the truth?"

'Ok, one question at a time. We know it's the truth because everything God said would happen thousands of years ago has happened exactly as He said it would. Our scriptures have a 100% success record. Everything Jesus said would happen is happening exactly as He said it would again 100% success record. Most people dismiss the scriptures as myths, fairy tales, and legends, but I ask one question. How many people have read the scriptures? Very few, they pass their opinions without having a clue as to what the scriptures actually contain. I throw you the challenge David examine the scriptures for yourself don't take my word or anyone else's word for it. Study the scriptures for yourself and check out the truth of what we are saying."

"Don't worry I intend to do exactly that. Where do you suggest I start my investigation?"

"Pastor Hussein is your man. He knows our Jewish scriptures and the Christian scriptures inside out. He was an Islam Mullah, a very devout Muslim before he became a Christian, so something important must have happened to change his mind. I will leave him to share his story with you himself. Meantime I will leave you to read a bit more, think you will find it all most interesting."

David had fallen asleep on the chair at the table, too tired to go to bed. Pastor Hussein wakened him with the offer of a nice hot cup of coffee. 'BOKER tov David, was your reading that interesting?"

"BOKER Tov pastor, it was certainly more interesting than I had expected" replied David as he yawned and stretched his muscles from sleep. "I have never found religion all that interesting in fact I usually find it very boring and totally irrelevant. What surprised me most was the way the Gentile scriptures speak about Israel. Are all these things going to happen in our country?" David had been amazed and fascinated at what he had read in the New Testament the pastor had loaned him.

"This battle of Armageddon....are you sure this guy didn't just have an over active imagination?" suggested David as he turned to the appropriate passage. "Are all these people just going to disappear like your book says, two men working in the field's one will be taken and one will be left. Two women going about their household tasks, one will be taken and one will be left. Two people may be lying in bed, one will be taken and one will be left.... It doesn't say where they will be taken to. Also I don't understand this antichrist, or that no one will be able to buy or sell without the mark either? It all sounds too far- fetched to be true if you ask me"

The pastor nodded understandingly. .... "Prophecy....It is much too close to the truth for comfort. You must understand the Book of Revelation was written two thousand years ago. Here is an interesting question for you, how could any mere man possibly have predicted the future as accurately as described in Revelation unless it had been revealed to him by the Living God, who knows all things? That's what prophecy is.... It is simply foretelling of future events."

"Your chart worries me, I admit that" said David. "What else do the prophets say about the future?"

"Where were you born David?"

"Hadassah University Hospital Jerusalem. Why?

The pastor thought for a moment "That makes you a Sabra Jew then, an Israeli born in Israel"

"Yes..."responded David slowly.

"You have no idea how much of a miracle that statement is, have you?' Think about the history of Israel David. After the temple was destroyed by the Romans in 70 AD or the year 3430 in your Jewish calendar, your people were scattered to the four corners of the earth. Jews had no homeland, no status as a nation, no common language. Yet the Jewish nation still survived as a people, a race different from any other race, a people without a country. It is amazing is it not, that after two thousand years your people have been brought back from the four corners of the earth to become a nation again. With your own language revived exactly as the prophets said it would be. Israel was without a ruler, today there is a government with a ruler, your prime minister. Israel is the only nation in the Middle East to elect a government through democratic proportional representation.'

The pastor posed the question. "How could a nation as small as Israel survive if God had not been on your side how can you explain your country's existence otherwise? Israel should have been extinct by now, yet it is flourishing. Your people are rebuilding your cities, planting more trees, orchards, vineyards. Israel is self- sufficient in food, water, and every other important commodity. The scriptures state that Israel will never again be ruled over by Gentiles. If our scriptures say it then that settles it. However the rest of prophetic scriptures do not contain quite such good news, the world is desperate for peace, but peace cannot be found anywhere until the antichrist, the false prophet is destroyed by the Prince of Peace who is coming again"

"I know who you mean.....Jesus..... I've got that bit, I think, but who is this antichrist and false prophet that you speak of?" queried David.

"The antichrist is simply what it says, anti-Christ or anti-Christian. It is written in the book of Revelation that there was war in Heaven, Lucifer which means 'the shining one' became puffed up with pride and went to war against the creator of the universe. He lost and was thrown out of Heaven with a third of the angels. Jesus referred to him as Satan prince of the air, the god of this world. Satan's aim is very simple: to destroy every man woman and child on our planet earth. He especially hates Jews and Christians. He hates the Jews because he knew the Messiah would be born a Jew from the royal line of David. He had to try to destroy your race in an effort to stop the Messiah from coming to earth. He didn't succeed!! The Jews are still Gods chosen people and God isn't finished with Israel yet. Jews have suffered much in the past but there is a great deal more to come, because you Jews are a stubborn, proud, stiff necked people who will not accept YESHUA as your Messiah, at least not until He once again stands triumphant on the Mount of Olives. Only then will your people recognize Jesus as your Messiah. It's all written down clearly for those who will incline their ears to hear and their spiritual eyes to see"

"This Satan, is he a man? How do we recognize him" quizzed David. "And this false prophet, how will we recognize him?"

The pastor drew up a seat and sat at the table, "Satan was an archangel, one of only two mentioned in scripture. He was the anointed cherub until he 'got too big for his britches' as the Americans would say. He declared war on God and His loyal angels. Jesus said He saw Satan cast down to earth where he leads an army of fallen angels and makes war on God's saints. Jesus calls the fallen angels demons others principalities and powers. Demons are basically spirits who try to enter human bodies, by doing so they are able to destroy mankind forcing them into all manner of evil and wickedness. Read the gospels you will learn that much of Jesus ministry involved casting demons out of people. When disciples are filled with The Holy Spirit they too have the power to cast demons out of people. After the crucifixion Jesus appeared to His disciples with very explicit instructions, to go and make disciples of all nations. He said all power and all authority I give to you. Greater is He that is in you, than he that is in the world. I will never leave you nor forsake you. It is a relationship that YESHUA extends to every individual. This is His desire for you David that you should become a son of God. Oh my Satan hates Jews especially Messianic Jewish believers and Christians with a passion because we know Satan is our real enemy, not people. Satan uses people for his diabolical plans, because people don't know the truth they are simply pawns doing his bidding. One day the church of Jesus through The Holy Spirit is at last waking up. However, we can continue this conversation later we have a lot of details to cover so that you can return home safely"

Chapter 11

The sweat was trickling down the back of Simeon's neck. Yacov was getting more and more heavy. He managed to perch Yacov upright, and give him some water to drink. The shift in position helped. "Wake up Yacov we have to get out of here before these tunnels blow to kingdom come. Wait what was that? Did you hear that noise? Footsteps, quick further into this alcove." The noise got louder and louder, it sounded like a proverbial army was headed their way.

"Leave me here Simeon. I am just going to hold you back. One of us has to get back with these flasks. I can hold them off for a while"

"No I don't think so, no way am I leaving you here. They know we are in here, but not exactly where, we have a few tricks of the trade we can use yet. Let's surprise them it will take them hours to check all these different tunnels. Only problem is we don't have that long either, I've set the explosives to blow at 08 00 hrs. So we better shift and get out of here speedily. Quiet! Someone is coming our way. Stay here, not a sound. I will deal with this."

Simeon crawled out of his hiding place with great stealth, and caught two guards completely by surprise. He dispatched the one nearest him, snapping his neck with a single blow. He died instantly. Simeon wheeled round in a single motion and used his lethal commando knife to slice through the second guard's carotid artery. He too breathed his last. "That evens the odds a bit. Two down just a few hundred to go" Quipped Simeon. "Come on man, let's get out of here, it won't be long before more will be arriving on our tail. Put on this jacket and cap. Fast as you can, I will strip the other one, it should buy us a few vital seconds if need be. We are going to join in the search for us. The uniforms are not exactly tailor made, but hey, they will serve the purpose well enough"

They heard a lot of shouting in the distance, so went in the opposite direction. They came upon a flight of stairs, "going up" thought Simeon. "That will do us, we want to get to the top, and out into the fresh air" They had managed up two flights of stairs without encountering any other guards. Then they heard voices coming from a room at the head of the stairs. They both edged quietly forward until they could gain a better view. What they found both surprised and pleased them. It was a room comprised of TV monitors. This was obviously the security nerve centre of the entire complex. They observed for a few minutes as four men were frantically scanning CCTV monitors, trying to locate the intruders. Pulling his handgun from its holster and attaching the silencer to the muzzle, Simeon took aim and felled the four men in quick succession. The men in the room heard nothing and died where they sat, still hearing nothing. "Hmm, nice work." enthused Yacov. "No problem" replied Simeon "let's move and get out of here. First let me check these monitors though, there might be a quicker way up to the top and out of this dungeon". Simeon removed the guard from the seat where he lay dead slumped over the monitor. "Sorry pal my need is greater than yours" not in the least sorry for dispatching this guard to the nether world. He scanned the monitors quickly then said "there it is, that's our exit"

"Not so fast" uttered a strange voice behind them. "Turn around very slowly, weapons down, hands raised very high. Do not try anything rash, it would give me very great pleasure to shoot you both" The words were most certainly Arabic but with a very strange accent. However, best not to argue with a gun, so both men laid their weapons down, and turned around very slowly. Yacov glanced at Simeon who understood his telepathy perfectly. Yacov threw himself on the floor to the left and Simeon fell to the right. The well tried move served them well again as the guard was taken completely by surprise and hesitated for a fraction of a second. The delay was all the time Yacov and Simeon needed. Both men rolled on the floor and kicked the guards legs from under him knocking him to the floor. Yacov then thumped his victim's head hard off the stone floor with such force that the skull smashed like a ripe melon. A second soldier managed to utter a yelp before Simeon could dispatch him and his cry was enough to alert the others in the vicinity who came running at speed towards the control room. Yet another guard ran into the room smack into Simeon who managed to dispose of him with a lethal blow from his knife. The desperate activity in eliminating the three guards had an adverse effect on Yacov's injuries, now the pain was excruciating. No time to think, blank the pain out. They had to get out of here, and fast.

****

JORDAN SAFE HOUSE

David was a very thoughtful young man as he got ready for bed that evening. His head was simply swirling with all of this new information. How on earth can this Yeshua be our Messiah, yet how can I deny all of these prophetic utterances and words from our own scriptures, written and recorded thousands of years before Yeshua was born. I have no answers to these questions. The Dead Sea scrolls were discovered the very day Israel was declared a nation again in May 1948. The Romans left behind only ashes. Thousands of Jews lay dead, and thousands were taken into captivity. No Messiah would be able to trace their lineage all the way back in history to King David's time as this Yeshua did. "It is written there in black and white how can I argue with these verifiable facts" thought David. Michael had read out prophecies relating to Israel from the Christian scriptures. Yeshua was a Jew same as him, he had lived in Israel more than two thousand years ago. He left prophecies for his disciples saying Hashem would scatter Jews to the four corners of the earth, but at the end of time HE would return Jews back to their promised land. The Gentile scriptures stated Hashem was not finished with the Jewish race yet these scriptures record that Israel will be trampled upon by Gentiles until the 'Times of the Gentiles' have ended. Michael said that Hashem had made a covenant with Israel that couldn't be broken. He showed David the scripture in Jeremiah

Jeremiah chapter 31 v 35

"HE who appoints the sun by day to shine who decrees the moon and stars to shine by night who stirs up the sea so that its waves roar. The Lord Almighty is His name. Only if these decrees vanish from MY sight declares The Lord, will Israel cease to be a nation in MY sight."

Well I can't argue with that either, thought David. The sun is still shining, the moon still lights the sky every night. The stars are still up above. Even I know our nation could not survive unless The Almighty had been protecting our people, our fledgling nation, from the enemies who surround us on every side. They are sending hundreds of rockets into our Cities, towns, and neighbor hoods and no one dies. Houses and buildings reduced to rubble but the people are safe. Must ask my Dad about all this when I get home. Then David decided to see what had so impacted Rabbi Kaduri, that he gave his life to Yeshua before he died. He opened the book and began to read some more. The book captivated David he just could not put it down.Let's see if he can give me some answers thought David as he made himself comfortable and started to read. David had fallen asleep still reading into the early hours of the morning his notes were strewn all over the bed. Questions, questions, questions, lots of questions, no answers!!!! He groaned with pain when he tried to lift his neck, it was stiff from lying in the most awkward position all night. That and lack of sleep forced David to move more slowly than usual when Pastor Hussain called him for breakfast. "Good morning David and how are you today? Did you sleep well?"

"No not very well" mumbled David. "I was reading Rabbi Kaduri's book, and it has left me with more questions than answers. How can a Rabbi over 100 years of age believe that Yeshua was the Messiah?"

"Ah, now is that not the thousand dollar question?We can chat about these questions over breakfast, food first. We have plenty of food and plenty of time."

"Plenty of time for questions I hope, my head is pickled

with all the questions I have flying around my brain" replied David. Pastor Hussain simply chuckled. He found this whole scene thoroughly amusing. "Don't worry David it will all become clear soon enough. What would you like to talk about first, I am happy to talk about any subject, eat first and then talk how does that sound to you?"

"Great, I appreciate you taking the time to help me make sense of all of this. How do you know these scriptures are the truth and not some fairy tales some smart talking men have made up?"

"Now, that is a very good question to start with, as you know I had been an Imam for many years. We had managed to get rid of most of the Christians from Bethlehem, though we had to be careful as our community needed the revenue that all these millions of Christians brought to our towns every year. The Jews do not need the tourism industry as the Muslim communities do. Very innovative are you Jews. You find answers to all of our problems such as water shortages, and serious medical issues. However I had a very vivid dream one night, when Jesus appeared to me and asked why I was persecuting him. I just couldn't get this dream out of my mind, I had no peace until I started to investigate the claims the Christians made about this Jesus. I started to read the New Testament first, and started like you with my list of questions. I opened at random the book of John. It held me spell bound I just couldn't put it down. I read and read right to the end. I concluded this was either the truth, or the biggest con that had ever fallen on mankind. My premise was to try my very best to disprove the evidence. I like facts and verifiable evidence. I want to share with you this next piece of information but I need to be able to trust you. Can I trust you David? I mean really trust you?"

"Yes of course you can, I would never betray your confidence" replied a thoroughly surprised David.

"I believe Yeshua would like me to share this next piece of explosive information with you David. However, this is seriously dangerous information, and if it ever gets out into the wrong ears this could start world war 3 it is that serious. I ask you again, can I trust you?"

"Yes you can Pastor, I promise I never will breathe a word to anyone"

"Ok" Said Pastor Hussein, "I believe I can trust you. This house is a safe house tucked away in a little corner of no man's land. It is owned by some very rich, powerful, influential Christians who got hold of Jeremiahs scroll that Baruch his servant buried in a field with both their personal seals imprinted on the scroll. (Jer. Chap 32v 8-17) here you read it out to me. Now this scroll was discovered on two rolls of copper (March 14th 1952 at back of cave 3 at Qumran not too far from here in fact. The scroll was given to Robert Feather a metallurgist from Yorkshire in England, many years later. He also had journalistic experience and managed to unravel the enigma of Jeremiah's copper scroll. It was initially in Jordanian hands but they were willing to part with it to the Jewish authorities in return for a fresh water supply. You can live without oil my young friend but not fresh water. The Jewish engineers have managed to capture every particle of moisture, even when someone sneezes into the atmosphere, and transform it into water.Anyway, the scroll was unraveled, but much to everyone's surprise it wasn't a letter or a passage of scripture that was discovered, it was a TREASURE MAP. This map written in Hebrew could only be deciphered by an Israeli scholar who could read ancient Hebrew. Again it was a Messianic believer who was able to decipher and crack the code of the scroll. An American firefighter Jim Barfield came across this information and went on the hunt to decipher the clues and find what was hidden, where it was hidden, and why had it remained hidden until now."

"Wow said David this is like something straight out of an Indiana Jones film. Quick tell me. I just know this is the exciting part"

David jumped when he heard his name being called. It was Meara coming in to say goodbye. She and Amir were ready to drive into Jerusalem to contact Gershom at the hospital. She was obviously shy and nervous, wondering how she would cope with a very different culture from her own. "Meara, don't be nervous, my family will love you, especially when you tell them I am fine and will be home soon. Amir will go with you into the hospital, help you find Gershom and I will be able to come home soon and show you around our wonderful new capital city. What an adventure you are going to have. You will be perfectly safe. My family will look after you, so don't worry. Will you promise me?"

"I will try my very best David, I only have to remember I don't want to get married, I know your family will be desperate to hear news of you, so yes I can do this. I can work and look after myself perfectly well. You tell me it is safe. So yes, I choose to believe you, and not give into my fears"With that statement,

Meara turned, and waved, said goodbye to Pastor Hussain and walked with Amir to his car. This is the first day of the rest of my life she thought. Lord Jesus promised to never leave me, or forsake me. He has a good plan for my life so I will put my trust in Him.

Chapter 12

The walk back along the tunnel was painfully slow. Yacov was barely conscious and a dead weight. "Have to hurry up, I can hear them coming" thought Simeon. "This door is jammed can't get it opened. Yacov, can you hear me? Can you hold them off till I can get this door open?" Theadrenalin was pumping thru Simeon's blood stream, fear lending him extra strength as he yanked the door open. "Keep your head down!" Simeon opened fire on the two guards at the top of the stairway. "Now we can get through"The two Mossad officers mounted the stairs and flattened themselves as the explosive device ripped the stairs apart and left nothing more than a massive gaping hole, dust and debris everywhere. They climbed yet another flight of stairs, and another doorway. Thankfully the night air hit them as they rushed through the door. They found themselves on a roof top, trapped with nowhere to run. Both men looked at the twenty metre drop to the ground. There was only one way down. Simeon unwound the coil of rope in his pack. They would have to abseil off the roof and down to the ground. Quickly securing the rope attaching himself and Yacov, Simeon heaved himself and his injured partner off the roof and into the darkness. It seemed a long painful slow decent down to the ground with Yacov feeling like a ton weight attached to him but at long last his feet hit the ground and Yacov moaned in pain. He felt the cold air and shivered, asking where they were. "Not sure" replied Simeon teeth chattering with the cold "but I think we are safe for the moment at least, we just need to find our way out of this death trap and be long gone on our way home before this hell hole of death blows to kingdom come.

****

HADASSAH HOSPITAL JERUSALEM

Gershom had finished his hospital rounds for the day. There had been no time for lunch and he was famished. As he was walking towards the dining room his pager rang, Gershom thought about ignoring it at first, however realizing it may be important he answered it. The receptionist informed him he had a visitor at the front desk. When he reached the front desk, the only person Gershom saw was an extremely attractive, young, Arab female.

"Hello' said Gershom. "I am Doctor Lieberman. Can I help you?"

"Yes" said Meara quietly. "Is there somewhere quiet we can talk I have a message from David."

"DAVID!" exclaimed Gershom. This was the last thing he expected. "What do you know about my brother? Is he alive? Is he safe, is he injured. Please tell me where he is. Who are you?"

"Wait, hold up" said Meara giggling. "I can only answer one question at a time. David is safe, and very well. My name is Meara. I am a friend, and have come to deliver the message to you that he is staying with friends until it is safe for him to come home"

"Well Meara, you have no idea how glad I am to meet you. My name is Gershom. Let's go to a small restaurant where I usually have some lunch. We will not be disturbed there. You can tell me what on earth my little brother has been up to this time, and we can then go tell my Mum that her youngest son is safe and coming home. Tell me how is David, where on earth is he?"

Meara smiled, and Gershom thought what a beautiful looking girl this young lady was, stunning in fact. She had lovely thick dark hair that framed a small oval face, large dark expressive eyes, a small petite nose, a face that dimpled beautifully showing perfect white teeth when she smiled.

"David is absolutely fine, staying in a safe house close to the Jordan border. He is just waiting patiently, or should I say, very impatiently, until your parents think it is safe for him to come home. He is very impatient, not at all happy with his enforced confinement."

"He is safe that is all that matters. Our parents will be so relieved it has been a very worrying time for them. Tell me everything, then we can go and break the good news to Mum, she will be overjoyed."

Ruth was surprised when Gershom came home with a young lady, but cried with happiness and relief, when she realized David was safe and well. Josh whooped with delight when he heard the news. There was great jubilation and celebration in the Lieberman household that evening.

"Meara How can Josh and I ever thank you for helping our son to escape from those who were holding him prisoner, it was so brave of you, to leave your home, family and friends to come and tell us our son was safe. Will you stay here with us? Josh and I would love to have you stay with us until you are settled and decide what you would like to do in the future. I just can't wait to see David again. When can we see him?"

"We were not sure what would be best. We decided to leave that decision with David's family then pass a message to Pastor Hussein's son Amir. He is returning home tomorrow. David even admitted he is missing school."

"What do you think Josh. When can we get David home?"

"While you two lovely ladies have been chatting and getting to know one another I've been working on a plan to get David home. I can meet with Amir in the morning, when he has finished his business in town. We can then make further plans for David to come home with Amir. We will have a couple of cars with station op guys tailing Amir, just to be on the safe side. He is coming home. Of that we can be sure. Now we can celebrate. Meara, what would you like to do?"

"I would like to meet Doctor and MRS Solomon. Pastor Hussein arranged for me to stay with them. I have the address here" said Meara.

"Ok, let's have a look. HAMALKA St. That's not too far away from here, quite central in fact."

'I will walk Meara there," chipped in Gershom quickly.

It was a great deal later in the evening when Gershom walked Meara home via the 'scenic' route. He found her extremely attractive and Gershom was full of admiration for the dangerous risks she had taken to help David get free from the people who had kidnapped him. Gershom also found her extremely interesting to chat to in fact this young lady was very different from any other female he had ever met.

Meara meanwhile was quietly trying to absorb the very different experience of freedom to walk along a strange city street without a family member with her. It felt warm, safe, and very clean to her. She liked Gershom and all of David's family. Then Gershom asked her what she was going to do now.

'I am not sure yet" replied Meara. "Everything is so strange and different here. I have never seen anything like this in my entire life. Everyone wears such strange clothes, young people walk along hand in hand without a chaperone. The markets are open late can you just walk in and out without buying anything?"

Gershom chuckled, and said, "Absolutely! The vendors want you to come in and browse around, have a good look, and then they hope you will like some of their wares or goods enough for you to buy something, they are very good at helping you to part with your money believe me. They often assist me in parting with a fair amount of my salary every month, so don't say I didn't warn you! I guess everything must seem very strange to you here. Would you like me to show you around our city and see some of the popular land marks? You can trust me Meara I would never do anything improper. It would be one way of saying thank you from our very grateful family. We were all so frightened we would never see David again. I have some hours leave due from the Hospital would you like to go exploring tomorrow?"

"Yes please, I would like that very much" Meara knew instinctively she could trust Gershom, most people did. He listened carefully when people spoke to him, they were aware he was someone who cared, who was interested in them as people. He genuinely found people interesting, wanting to know what they thought, how they felt. It helped a great deal he was young, dark and handsome, most women found him attractive, and Meara was no exception.

The two young folk arranged to meet first thing the following morning. Gershom was looking forward to seeing Meara again. He knew he would have to be very patient with this particular young lady, build up a strong friendship first, gain her trust. However he was in no hurry, they were young, had all the time in the world. He rarely bothered with holidays, so he arranged a few days leave with ease. The hospital consultants were delighted when Gershom explained that David was alive and well and would be coming home soon. The news would be kept under wraps for the moment until David was safely home again.

The following morning was bright and sunny, as usual, when Gershom arrived to take Meara out for the day.

"Hope you have good strong walking shoes on today, it is much easier to walk around old Jerusalem with decent walking shoes;stiletto heels are not at all advised.It is only a square mile, but there is a lot to see, if you want to look at all four areas. It would be better to split the areas up and not try to see everything in the one day."

"I don't mind where we go, or how far we walk. I am just so excited to be here, walking freely on my own no relatives with me. It just feels so totally surreal. I love this. Thank you for willing to be my guide today, I fully appreciate my arrival has disrupted your well-ordered routine."

Gershom was caught by Meara's sheer exuberance, and excitement. "I keep forgetting this is all so new for you it must be a bit overwhelming. Would you like to eat first? There are many Deli' type places and cafe's near the Jaffa gate. The food is always fresh and well prepared, reasonably priced as well" They strolled along Ben Yehuda Street towards the Jaffa gate. Meara was simply excited by everything she saw, and because Jaffa gate was at the top of a pretty steep climb they had a magnificent view all the way down to the lower levels towards the Souk. The market was fairly bustling with life, everyone was busy with work, going somewhere, coming from somewhere, and Meara was surprised at how quickly she felt she belonged here. No one took any notice at all, of the pretty young lady. She blended in with the busy folks in the market place. What did surprise Meara was when she noticed Arab traders on one side of the Souk and Jews on the other side often chatting to each other, drinking tea and coffee together. They were obviously friends with each other. No signs of tension at all. They simply lived their lives in harmony. In the pedestrian area at the top of the Souk a young lady was playing her harp in the sunshine. The music was absolutely beautiful, and many folks were sitting around, strolling, browsing, chatting, eating at one of the many open air cafe's enjoying the sunshine. Meara had hundreds of questions and wanted to know everything yesterday.

However Gershom got his own back when he watched Meara, highly amused as she tried to eat falafel in Pitta bread. The falafel is a deep fried ball of seasoned chickpea paste with onions, wheat, flour and garlic, with as much diced salad and vegetables as will fit the pocket and smothered with various sauces of your choice. It is a great favourite snack in Israel, very healthy, but with a knack to eating it without spilling a mess everywhere. The trick is to nibble from the top and not the sides. Gershom showed Meara how once he stopped laughing at the mess she was making.

"Never mind, in a few days with plenty of practice, you will be snacking on falafel like a native" he said. "You must always remember the cardinal rule and drink plenty of water it is so easy to become dehydrated in the heat. You will get used to it pretty quickly though. When we finish our snack I thought we could go have a look at the Austrian Pilgrim Hospice. It gives an amazing panoramic view over the whole city, even better you don't have to climb the stairs up to the top as it has a lift, a beautiful roof café, superb food and home baking guaranteed you will love this, and it is so quiet. A little piece of Vienna with the best apple strudel you will ever taste, mmm making my mouth water just the thought of what awaits us. It was built almost 200 years ago for visitors and Pilgrims in 1863 in fact it's the oldest guesthouse in the Old City. There are many very old photographs lining the walls showing us the history of Jerusalem, then and now.

"That sounds lovely, can we go now? I want to see everything." It didn't take long for them to reach the Hospice. They found it tucked in a little corner between the Lion gate and Damascus gate, at the Via Dolorosa intersection. It can be pretty busy during the day as there will usually be groups of Pilgrims and tourists following in the last footsteps of Jesus of Nazareth as he carried the cross to Golgotha where He was crucified. Meara was simply astounded at the teeming life of the old city. Everyone bustling about, busy traders trying to sell their wares to the many tourists willing to buy trinkets, relics, jewelry, plates, Holy Land gifts, oils, spices, photographs, shofars. However these items tend to be cheaper to buy out-with the Old City. Gershom promised he would take Meara to Mahane Yehuda market where everything was on sale cheaper there.

The view from the top of the hospice across The Old City took Meara's breath away. Gershom realized they were not leaving anytime soon so he settled in for the long haul. However it also gave him the opportunity to find out a bit more of what this lovely young ladies life had been like before she met his little brother.

"What was your life like growing up? Do you miss your family? Of course you do, silly question."

Meara had the loveliest smile thought Gershom, but listened as she tentatively began to explain what her early life had been like growing up in a traditional Arab household. I had nine sisters and one brother. My older sisters are all married now except Sara, she and I have always been very close friends, separated by Karim my older brother and always fathers favourite child. I used to be jealous of him because he got everything he wanted. At such a young age I had not realized in our culture male and female are considered so differently. The worst time came when Sara started her menstrual cycle and was now eligible for marriage. Father had chosen an older man, 50 at least to be Sara's husband. He wanted a young bride to give him more sons. It was terrible, Sara did not want to marry him, but fathers have full rights to dispose of their daughters in any marriage they saw fit. My mother tried to intervene on Sara's behalf, but father dismissed her, there was nothing she could do. I realized then what it was like to be a woman in our culture."

"Did you not have any say in your future, or your education?

"No, not at all Girls are married as young as fourteen, often as third or fourth wives depending on how rich the groom to be is. A wife belongs to her husband, she is his property, to deal with or dispose of as he wishes. Islam gives men the right to divorce a wife without any reason or motive, though women cannot divorce men. The men simply say "I divorce you three times in the presence of two male witnesses, and the divorce is final in a matter of minutes"

"Then what do you do? Can you work, get a job of some sort? I sure can't imagine this happening to any Jewish girl I know, the girl would take him for every penny he owned. He would literally end up penniless and he would have to move away from the neighbor-hood, he would be shunned otherwise. Our women are fierce, they sure stick together, and they serve two years in the army the same as the men, Arab men don't like the fact that we have female soldiers in our army, they believe they cannot be accepted into heaven if they are killed by a female soldier"

Meara chuckled at that statement "Our women are not often educated to a very high standard. They usually get married young have babies quickly so why waste time and money on education? Things are changing now though, as women are at home all day and can watch television while men are out working, so they are becoming much more interested in the world outside our small villages.The only education many of our women have is to learn The Koran by rote. A female tutor sounds it out, and the girls learn by repetition. We learn early in life, boys are kings in their mothers lives, fathers have very little to do with their daughters, simply send messages through a third or fourth wife. Females very rarely go out in public, never ever alone without being veiled, which makes walking difficult and crossing the road even more hazardous. She must also be accompanied by a male, even her own son, providing he is 9 years of age"

"Now I am shocked, I simply cannot imagine any boy of 9, or any boy of any age, telling my mother what to do. My goodness she would send him packing with a clip round the ear. Our women rule the roost in our homes. Believe me, we men know our place. What shocked me initially though was how you found the courage to leave your home, your family your village. Our life here must seem like you have landed on another planet, never mind just another part of the same country" stated a bemused Gershom.

"I love reading books, and have read every book I could get my hands on since I was very young. I knew from many of the books I read that life was very different for women in other countries and other cultures. I just didn't appreciate how different! But I think I will get used to it. I just love the fact that I am virtually invisible here no one would ever recognize me. I feel free Gershom. For the first time in my entire life I feel free. It is the most amazing feeling. It was my grandmother who opened my eyes to the different life I could have. My happiest hours were spent at my grandmother's home. She was old so no one bothered with her. She was also widowed, considered too old for marriage. I was a 'troublesome child' who had great fun playing all sorts of horrible pranks on my brother. He got into terrible trouble. We did call a truce, but I became more and more of a rebel and somewhat of an embarrassment to my father, I was often punished and given the most menial tasks to do, that is how I met David. He did his best to talk to me, and help with chores, he also made me laugh I just knew he would never hurt me, so we ended up talking about many things. He opened my eyes to the world outside our small village. I liked David very much however I never dreamed that I could escape the life I was living and end up talking to you in Jerusalem. I have to pinch myself to make sure I am not dreaming all of this."

"No way, are you dreaming this Meara. We are in Jerusalem and you are telling me what you would like to do with the rest of your life. You are very different from any other Arab lady I have met, but first things first what would you like to do now you can go and do whatever you would like. The world really is your oyster. Would you like to continue with your education, get a job, or what?"

"I think I would most like to teach young children, especially young Arab girls. Only in this way, through education, can thousands of women of the Muslim faith be free from the life of bondage that they have to live. However to pay for my education, I will have to get a job of some sort. I am not sure what I can do, but I can work hard and I am willing to learn."

"Ok, let's think, what are you good at?" asked Gershom. "What do you like doing?"

"Just the usual things I guess like cooking, cleaning, serving master and his guests, looking after the little ones, playing games, and singing songs. These were some of my happiest times, and I liked teaching some of the older girls how to read so they too could understand how vast, how amazing our planet is, what is happening in the world out- side our small village. That is when I realized I loved education and teaching younger children to read, write and count."

"Well now, you are a determined young lady with a mind of your own, so whatever you decide to do, you will be successful. I know my parents will help you with whatever you decide as will Doctor and MRS Solomon. They have a secure network of friends who help and support each other, so no fear, they will help with your education, and you can help with the children or whatever suits you best in between your studies. I will always be around to help you study, your language skills are very good, you obviously have a good ear for languages, now that would be a great job for you, we Jews and Arabs certainly need some good interpreters, they sure don't hear each other too well!!!!! There is no rush Meara. This has been a huge shock for you it will take time to adjust. You will need time to acclimatize to our country, get to know us better. We really aren't such a bad lot once you get to know us"

"I like you all very much, everyone has been so very kind and helpful, but surely you are too busy with your important work to waste time showing me around your lovely city."

"Not at all, I am realizing how little leisure time I actually use. I would love to spend more time helping you get used to our quirky ways of doing things. I am looking forward to it already."

"Thank you Gershom, I really appreciate your offer. Everything is certainly very strange. You all seem to do everything together. There are no separate quarters for male and female in any of the homes I have been in, you all eat together, talk as equals, everyone freely share theirthoughts and opinions. Rebekah, freely shares her opinions and thoughts with her parents, Doctor and MRS Solomon. I like her she has been so kind allowing me to share her room. I haven't met Michael, Doctor and MRS Solomon's son, yet. He is often away with IDF duties. Everyone has made me feel very welcome. I can't believe how free I feel here. It feels good Gershom I know I made the right decision helping David to escape. How wonderful to be here when your family all meet up again."

"Believe me, without you it would not have happened, and I would not have had the pleasure of showing you around our crazy city, so where would you like to go next?"

"I would love to go to the Mount of Olives, The Garden of Gethsemane, and The Garden Tomb. I would like to see Gate Beautiful the Wailing Wall and the Temple Mount. I would like to join all of you on Friday evening for the celebration of Shabbat. I would like to see all around The City of David, whew!I don't mind where we go I'm just so excited to be here and seeing all of it"

"Ok Let's go to Mount of Olives first, the view is awesome from the top. We can hop on the bus that will save us the hard climb up to the top of the mount. Then we can slowly walk down, it's easier seeing everything from the highest point. We have lot's to see so let's get started."

Chapter 13

"Well Young David, are you ready to hear my exciting news? You know in Jeremiah chapter 32 v 9 to the end of the chapter that Jeremiah buried a scroll in the plot of land he bought from his cousin. We also know he was taken into captivity and carried off to Babylon by Nebuchadnezzar in 586 BC. And the TEMPLE was destroyed that same year. The book of Daniel tells us that The Jews returned home to Israel 70 years later in the year 538 BC. It is all thoroughly well documented in your own scriptures. You are reading it for yourself now. We also know the second temple was built by Nehemiah and Zerubbabel. Jesus died at 33 years of age. HE was crucified outside the city walls. If you turn to the Christian scriptures, in book of Matthew chapter 24 YESHUA/Jesus said the second temple would be destroyed and we know it was by the Romans 37 years after the crucifixion exactly as Jesus said it would be. So now we have an accurate time line to follow. Everything is thoroughly well documented since then. However the Dead Sea scrolls were found the very same day Israel was declared a nation by a young Bedouin boy called Mohamed el-Dib, in caves of Qumran. He threw a stone into a cave and it clinked against something. When he went to investigate he found many stone jars. He hadn't a clue what he had found so he ran for a friend who helped him to carry some of the jars back to their tribe. My goodness these scrolls went half way round the world. Many ended up sold to American dealers, though initially they were offered to a cobbler come antiquities dealer named Khalil ESCANDER SHANIN who operated in Jerusalem.

They were mostly sold to scholars from America who offered more money than anyone else. Some of the scrolls were sold to KANDO the Armenian. Some other scrolls were bought by Max Athanasius Samuel he recognized the language as Hebrew. He asked Tavia Wechsler a Jewish friend if he understood the script and was surprised at his friend's reaction he became most excited and asked if he could take them to President MAGNES of Hebrew University. The Head of the Archaeology Dept. was El SUKENIK. This was in Nov 1947.As history noted, all the surrounding Arab countries were arrayed against the fledgling Israeli country, however against all odds Israel won that war and their independence.

El SUKENIK consulted his son General YIGAEL YADIN who brought back the second group of scrolls from the merchant in Bethlehem. This batch contained the Isaiah scroll. The date..... November 29th 1947... the VERY DAY the Partition of Palestine was voted by The United Nations. NOW Israel was a nation in its own right. Back staying in their own land never again to be uprooted from the land Hashem, Almighty God gave them. This is your history David your Covenant keeping God kept Covenant. Israel today is a proud, leading, prosperous nation. You are living in the days of Elijah indeed.

You know this David. How could this possibly ALL be coincidence? How on earth could a nation of only a few thousand people possibly go to war against every surrounding nation and win against overwhelming odds. You only had a couple of clapped out fighter planes, and a couple of tanks. Your soldiers were for the most part book lovers, Doctors, lawyers, Professors, highly educated, but hardly handy with weapons, guns, driving tanks, warfare tactics. They had to learn to till the land, grow produce, plant crops, trees, plants, flowers, herbs in a dessert terrain. The remnant coming out of the concentration camps were shell shocked, beaten, demoralized scared. Many of the men had never held a weapon in their lives. They were emaciated and exhausted. They must have felt they had exchanged one kind of hell for another. With one difference, they were free. They could not go back, there was no- where else for them to go so they would plant their crops, build up their communities live in kibbutz. They built new homes, hospitals, and schools. I have always admired Israeli's. Out of sand and malaria ridden swamps you have built one of the strongest nations in our world today.

However what else did The Copper Scroll reveal to us? This is the most exciting part. It was actually noted by a Christian guy called Jim Barfield. The scroll had been unraveled by an English guy called Robert Flowers, a metallurgist to trade. Now we know it is a TREASURE MAP. It has taken many years to find out exactly where the treasure is hidden. What can the treasure possibly be? You are here in this cottage because some American Christians have worked out the clues and they know we are at this moment in time very close to this treasure. They are not allowed anywhere near the site because it is in a very sensitive area between the Arab side and Jewish side of the divide. However long story cut short, Jim has a Christian friend who owns a business developing scanners for all sorts of purposes. He suggested using the developed scanners for space exploration. These scanners are no ordinary scanners they are massive round orbs in size, but ideal for having a look see what is very deeply hidden underground in this area. Obviously this is pretty hush hush, but you know what archaeologists are like, they are as nosy as the next guy. The Government would not allow anyone near this area but a member of the Knesset was willing to take a chance and have a look. Only he could get near the sight as there are cameras and drones all around the area. They would frazzle anyone who went near this site without permission however he received the permit and agreed to have a look. In the early hours of the morning when everyone else was asleep he went scanning with a small but very powerful scanner strapped to his back.Ah David, you have never experienced such excitement as we experienced that night!"

"Ok Quick, I am still waiting patiently for you to give me a clue!"

"Patience, I am coming to the exciting part. The area known as Hill of KOHLITT is where the excitement begins. The scanner suddenly developed a mind of its own and it went crazy, lighting up with every colour of the rainbow, jumping birling turning like a giant cartwheel itbounced all over the place, with loud screeching bleeping. Man alive what excitement in the camp that night. All the colours were sparking denoting gold, silver, platinum, precious stones. The scanner went into overdrive, worse than any polytechnic display you will see at a Walt Disney park in Florida. Now that is some sight if you have never seen it.The tech guys were struggling to keep up with all of the information flying off the pages. At least 60 different sites were located. The antiquities archaeologists are pretty much one hundred percent sure that is where the Temple Vessels have been hidden for thousands of years. Ever since Jeremiah hid them down there before the children of Israel were taken into captivity by the Babylonians."

"Oh man, are you sure?" David was awestruck and excited all at the same time. He knew exactly what this meant for Israel. The THIRD TEMPLE would be built. So this is what Rabbi KADURI knew before he died. "Now I understand," said David. "So what is going to happen next?"

"Nothing is going to happen. Not at the moment anyway. The Prime Minister has stated very firmly that the treasure cannot be brought up to the surface as this truly would spark the Third world war. Every Arab country all over the world would come against our nation. Read your scriptures young David, EZEKIEL chapter 37, tells you the Jews will return to their land in the latter days. That happened in 1947. (Fifty years later, after another Jubilee year) and after yet another war Jerusalem was captured from the Jordanian army and returned to Israel. Jerusalem is once again capital of Israel. Now the Temple vessels have been located and the temple will be rebuilt. This is my opinion David so do not quote me on this one. After chapter 37 of Ezekiel comes chapter 38 and chapter 39. Have a read of these chapters and I will make a cup of tea, this has been a lengthy discourse. Are you fed up yet?"

"Absolutely not, no way, I fully appreciate how important this information is for our nation. Can I at least share it with my parents? I feel they need to know this as well. They will get it Pastor Hussein, they can be trusted."

"Of course David, you know we are living in amazing days. I am giving you this information fully as I believe God is asking me to trust you to take this information back and warn your family these are the days we are living in. Get ready, get prepared. The war of EZEKIEL chap 38 and 39 will happen. The countries even now are plotting together. IRAN SYRIA and RUSSIA are coming together and making their foul plans to wipe us all out. Right now Russia is aggrieved that Israel has found trillion of cubits of both gas and oil in the Leviathan field close to Haifa. That alone makes you a player in the world stakes. A very small nation, already rich and then you find gas and oil. Already you are building a pipeline down through Cyprus and then through into Greece, supplying all the lower Mediterranean islands and countries. This seriously affects Russia's economic situation, and cuts her revenue by a large margin. Again Scripture names the nations that will come to war against you. GOG and MAGOG is Russia. PERSIA is Iran, Iraq. CUSH is Sudan and Somalia. PUT is Libya. TOGORMAH is Turkey. GOMER is generally recognized as Germany. TYRE and SIDON is Lebanon. TEMAN is Yemen. SHEBA DEDAN and TARSHISH is Saudi Arabia.However, Michael the Archangel will once again with the warrior angels come and save Israel from total annihilation. That is not the end David. Hopefully you and your family will accept YESHUA as your SAVIOUR and you will be RAPTURED. Now! It is time for tea, I know this is a lot to take in, but it is extremely important you have this information. Time is short. Our God is a Covenant keeping God. Guess who wins the war. Yep you guessed it, Our God. You have to read the last pages of The Christian Scriptures to understand what is going to happen next. Our God does nothing without warning His prophets first. You have been called by Hashem to warn your family of these truths. Many thousands of young Jews are becoming Messianic believers. They are warning your politicians of things to come. Some of your politicians already know these facts, a number of your government ministers meet up with Messianic believers to study the scriptures every Friday afternoon before Shabbat to pray and ponder these things. Here is your tea. I will give you a Bible and a photo copy of some of my own notes to take home with you. Read and study David take pages and pages of your own notes. You need to keep reference. Now come, enough for today. I have a Bible study to prepare for tonight. Amir returns home tomorrow so you should receive good news as to when you can return home"

Chapter14

"Well now lovely lady, Look at you!" Gershom was rather taken aback when Meara answered the door this morning. She was excited and all ready for another day of getting to know this fascinating city. Her hair was fashioned in a different style, and it suited her new look.

"Ok, so tell me what has happened to you? It suits you very well, though, you look lovely today" "Thank you, my friend Rebekah has taken me in hand. We are very similar in age and size so she suggested I try on some of her clothes and see what ones I liked and suited. Before I met David I had never worn a pair of trousers before, but these light denim trousers are very comfortable, and the pink top is also very comfortable. It is a great joy to look around and see everything, experience the different smells of spices, vegetables. Look in shop windows and see the lovely jewelry, bracelets, matching necklace and ear rings. I am enjoying my new life Gershom. It's all so new and exciting. Where are we going today?"

"Now that you have your new travel pass it is so easy to travel round the city. Keep it safe, you have to top it up every so often, with it you can hop on and off the trams and buses as often as you like. However the children watch like hawks to make sure you use your pass to pay for your ride, and not try to dodge paying. Believe me they will call you out on it.I just give my pass to one of the kids they love to 'ding' it for you. The trams come along every few minutes so it is very easy to get around the city. Why don't we take the bus up to the Mount of Olives, we haven't been there yet?"

"Oh wow, what a view over the whole city. The bumpy ride to get here was well worth the discomfort. I can't believe how clean, beautiful and quiet it is here. There is hardly a sound from the few groups of people who are here. They are probably as astonished as I am. This is just amazing Gershom. Thank you for bringing me up here, I would never have found this on my own"

"I honestly did not appreciate how beautiful this area was. It really is a lovely area with a very special atmosphere of its own. I've never experienced this before. I guess it is a very Holy place. Why is it so special to Christians?"

"This is the place where Jesus came most often with His disciples. He explained what would happen in the future after he died. We are that future, these things that Jesus foretold are happening in our time right now. It would be impossible to be this detailed and this accurate more than 2000 years ago if He did not know ahead of time what was going to happen. Let's sit here in this quiet spot and I will read out His words. I have my Bible in my bag. This is from the first book of the Christian scriptures in Matt chapter 24. Jesus and His disciples had just left the Temple. That was when your Jewish Temple was still standing in magnificent splendor. The disciples wanted to show Jesus all the magnificent buildings of The Temple, when Jesus next comment shocked them.

"Do you not know that The Temple and every single building attached to the Temple will be totally destroyed and not one single stone will be left one on top of another when the destruction is finished. The disciples were shocked at this statement and asked The Master when would this happen, and what other signs should they look for.

Gershom said, "We know that The Temple was destroyed by Titus and The Jews were wiped out. Many Jews were taken to Rome as slaves and servants of the Roman Legion. But what were the other signs Jesus told his disciples to look for?"

Meara continued to read. "There will be wars, and rumours of wars, there will be Famines, Pestilences, plagues, horrible diseases. There will be earthquakes, fires landslides and tsunamis. However, the worst will come many centuries from now. Everything will happen around Jerusalem. The Jews will be back in their own land, and Jerusalem will one day be capital again of Israel. Jesus knew His scriptures and told His disciples this was all explained in the book of Daniel, chapter 9 through to the end. This is all recorded in your own scriptures Gershom"

"Hmm I can see I will be up all night reading our scriptures checking out the truth of all this. Did Jesus say all that before He was crucified? All these things are happening right now as we speak. They only happened a few years ago. I well remember my dad telling us of the excitement that night when our army under Moshe Dayan managed to rout Jerusalem from the Jordanian army. My parents were there and my dad shared it with me one evening. What excitement in the whole country, the singing, dancing, great celebration. No one went home they were all much too excited to think about sleep. Now today you are saying that Jesus prophesied all these things. They are written in the Christian scriptures"

"They are all here, have a look for yourself. The book of Revelation is very interesting it talks of rivers turning blood red. Many rivers are turning blood red today I remember Pastor Hussein talking about the river in Indonesia, In Cusco, Peru. Even in Mecca along with plagues of locusts. They have never seen plagues of locusts like this before, eating every single green sprig and shoot causing famine and death on a scale they could never imagine in their worst nightmares. There is also drought, earthquakes, hurricanes, tornadoes, flooding, bush fires, rain forests, volcanic eruptions, countries seeing snow for the first time, the corona virus of course. Not enough clean, fresh water to drink, never mind to shower and wash hands. Millions of people are dying today Gershom. Jesus warned His disciples this would all happen, but not to fear He was coming back to claim His own and we would go to be with Him"

"I have never heard of any of this until now, I am reading the words for myself. I can't understand why no one has shared any of this with us before now, surely our Rabbis have heard of this?"

"Jesus said none of this would happen 'until the times of the 'Gentiles have ended'. My understanding from Pastor Hussein's teaching was. When Israel became a nation, the time line changed from a gentile time clock back to the Jewish time clock. Daniel explains that better than I ever could, here read for yourself, it's from your scriptures. You can also count better than I can so I will leave you to count up the years. It is future, but it certainly fits in with what is happening today. The Third Temple will be built Gershom. Scripture says it so that settles it. I am glad I have a pretty good idea of what is going to happen though. At least we can be prepared and not waste the time we have.

Everything is going so fast, and it is all playing out exactly as the Scriptures have it documented. Down there, is the Garden of Gethsemane, we can walk there can't we Gershom? I would love to just slowly wander around, and imagine Jesus talking to His disciples"

Meara went for a walk on her own leaving Gershom to read more of the Book of Daniel. The sunshine was glorious and the garden very quiet, and peaceful. Gershom became totally engrossed with the way scripture seemed to open his understanding of his beloved nation, how much of a miracle it all was, how much Hashem truly loved His Jewish sons and daughters. He protected them and gave them victory in the many wars they have had to fight since becoming a fledgling young nation. However the information was also causing a great deal of confusion. He jumped when Meara tapped him on the shoulder and stated she would like to try another falafel.

"Ok I'm getting hungry as well, just let me finish reading this last section then we can walk down to the old town. Who is this son of perdition, this man of lawlessness, this man of sin? He sounds quite a character"

"I remember Pastor Hussein telling us he was the antichrist. He has not come thru yet, but is being kept very well hidden until it is time for him to appear. In fact Dr. Solomon was telling us all about that person in our study session last week. You should ask him these questions, he is very knowledgeable, and will be able to answer all your questions much better than I ever could. Your Mum is coming along to the study as well. She and MRS Solomon have become very good friends since David was abducted. Amir said he and David are coming back tomorrow. Your mum is so excited Gershom. It will be so good to see David I guess he will find me very much changed since I last saw him"

"All of our lives have been turned upside down since my little brother's last escapade, but you are right it will be wonderful to see him again. What's the bet my mum will be cooking and baking all of his favourite foods' It will be quite a feast, and all down to you Meara being brave enough to help him escape, he could not have done it without your help"

"Are you kidding, I am having the most wonderful time of my life Gershom, I had no idea places like this existed. Everything has been amazing so far, and there is so much to explore and experience yet. I want to sing and dance, smell the roses and different flowers, taste the food and spices. I am actually exploring and walking through the garden of Gethsemane, imagine, it was here thousands of years ago in exactly the same place, and we get to follow in Jesus footsteps"

Gershom smiled and held out his hand to Meara. It seemed the most natural thing in the world to take his hand and walk with him.

Chapter 15

Judy Harriman took a deep breath before knocking on Joshua Lieberman's office door. She couldn't for the life of her figure out what she had done wrong this time, must have been something serious to have been called to the chief's office. A summons like this usually meant a stiff reprimand, thought Judy.

"Enter!" commanded a deep male voice. As the door opened Josh looked up from the mountain of paperwork cluttering his desk, noting the beautiful young woman dressed in a pale blue tracksuit complete with matching training shoes. "Judy, take a seat. You are probably wondering why I brought you here. I have a proposition to put to you, actually it's an assignment somewhat out-with your usual remit, but I very much believe that you are the right person for this particular task.'

Judy sat back somewhat relieved yet intrigued at the same time. "What do you have in mind sir?"

"It has been brought to my attention that you are a trained medic, leader of your team, with your specialist area being the field of viral epidemiology of viral infections. Your thesis was impressive, as was your doctorate. However the important fact also was the time your unit spent in Syria when the president of Syria fired off some chemical weapons during the war situation there. Your team went in to help the children seriously affected, and bring them down to our medical facilities in Israel. Many children were saved by your team intervention. They would have died otherwise. Can I be frank with you Judy? We have a very dangerous ops situation unfolding as we speak. Two of our top operatives have gone up there to try and find some of this deadly toxin that we know they have hidden deep down in the maze of tunnels on our Northern border. It is the deadliest virus yet our enemies are planning on firing into our towns and cities. We simply must find a sample of this virus and the genetic code, otherwise our nation will have no protection when this lethal virus hits. All we know is that our guys are in and on their way out with samples. We are in touch with the Kurds operating up there but we need our own team on the spot to bring them back. Would you be willing to go back into the danger zone to do that Judy?"

"Yes sir, of course. It's what I am trained to do. This virus, does it have a name?"

"It does, it's called Matreus. It's an extremely nasty and very fast acting haemorrhagic virus that causes death in a matter of hours. The sooner we can get samples of it with the genetic code then the virologists can get to work producing a safe vaccine that will give our people a chance.Can you assemble your team and be ready in a couple of hours? Our boys are in trouble up there Judy, but you are our best chance, I am banking on you to get them back to safety"

"Will do sir, we will do our best you know that. The Kurds are great. They help us as much as possible. They can go places we can't. They also know their people will need protection from this virus as well. We have the means and facilities to beat this, our scientific minds have always been in the forefront of this type of thing. Ok, we will be off shortly. Will that be all Sir?"

"Yes, thank you Judy, best of luck, we will catch a debrief when you return"

****

SYRIAN UNDERGROUND WEAPON DEPOT

The search light flared from the tower. Simeon shivered with cold and tension as he backed up against the wall. He was soaking with perspiration the sweat breaking out along his hairline and trickling down his neck.

"Shhhh" He said, as he pulled Yacov's arm, forcing him to a crouching position. "Get down flat, and slither along as close to the wall as quietly as you can. We have to stay out of sight. If that search light beam catches us, we will be toast" The two agents skirted the wall quietly, swiftly, the rocks scraping and tearing the skin from their hands and knees. The night air was bitterly cold both men were freezing and trying to stop their teeth from chattering.

Simeon looked at the luminous dial of his watch. Time was closing in on them. The whole place was going to blow in less than 30 mins. They had to be well away from there before then. The difficulty was the whole area was now swarming with armed guards. They could hear loud voices shouting to each other, orders being barked out, heavy booted feet running. They heard alarms ringing in the distance, the siren blaring, the searchlight sweeping to and fro.

Then they heard the shout! Simeon glanced back, they had been seen. Simeon fired, the guard buckled and fell. "Now Yacov, run!" They ran on twisting and weaving, hearing the boots clattering behind them. Yacov was sluggish, his whole body racked with pain. His legs felt like lead, his breath rasping. He stumbled and fell rolling down a hill andslithered over ragged rocks that tore the skin, until he landed in a foul smelling ditch. Simeon followed him, dodging the machine gun fire that swept back and forth, bullets ricocheting everywhere. Simeon threw a grenade that exploded in the middle of the first group of guards. That bought them a little time.

Yacov had passed out, so Simeon hauled him into a sitting position, laid his weight across his back and heaved himself upright lifting Yakov in a crude fireman's lift. He jogged and walked, jogged some more, his knees buckling under the weight. Then he had to stop to draw breath. Simeon was making for trees that would afford them some cover and shelter. Yacov moaned. "Yacov, wake up!! Can you hear me?" "Tired, I'm so tired and cold Simeon. Leave me here and you get back to base. You need to get back I will just hold you up"

"No way Yacov I am not leaving you here. You are coming back with me. We have to keep moving though, this whole place is going to blow in less than 15 minutes, and if we are not out of here we blow with it, so we had better get moving. Yacov, can you hear me. Can you walk if you lean on me?"

"I will try, help me up and let's go"

Simeon pulled Yacov's good arm round his shoulder, and half carried, half dragged his friend into the forest. He had to ignore his own pain, and try to staunch the flow of blood that had started to flow from the bullet wound, but he was losing it, he felt light headed, and dizzy, his vision becoming blurred.

He had to push on, one foot in front of the other. They were both weakening, gasping, for breath ragged breathing. "How much further now Simeon?"

"Not too far now. Keep going. One step more, another step, walk. That's it come on you can do it. Don't cut out on me now. We have to be further away than this before the whole enchilada blows. Simeon glanced at his luminous watch, only 7 more minutes. "We can make this Yakov" Just then they heard the sound of a twig snapping, footsteps were moving towards them, ever closer.

"Shhh---quiet, get down!" ordered Simeon.

Chapter 16

"ARE you all to go home David? You will be excited at the prospect of seeing your family again. It has certainly been an adventure for you. We have covered many thoughts, facts, and topics over these last few days. You have much to ponder and a good bit of study ahead of you. I haveone more thought to share with you before you leave, the only piece of advice I can give you....

Think of a baseball game the Americans are so fond of, or cricket that the English are crazy about. It is a game of two opposing teams who hit the ball and try to score as many runs as possible before they are all knocked out. Now look at this metaphor spiritually, it looks as if the team of Satan and his demons are clocking up lots and lots of runs and are winning, but the secret is this. Listen carefully, the church of Jesus the Nazarene has not been into bat yet, that is coming soon and I have read the very last page of the book. The next secret I am going to tell you is....... Guess who wins? Our God wins, Satan loses, game set and match and is thrown into the lake of fire God has prepared for him and all of his followers.

Therefore I say this to you my young friend: choose which team you want to be a part of. Me? I always like to be on the winning team! To finish off this session, I have much work to do. Just supposing for arguments sake, this is all complete and utter nonsense. You know it is not, but can you afford to take that chance. I am an old man now coming to the end of my life. If I die and find there is nothing, then I have lost nothing. However if you reach the end of your life and discover this was the truth, that you disregarded this information, that will then mean you have lost everything!!Think carefully young David. investigate thoroughly, it is the most important decision you will ever make in your life, your decision in this matter determines where you will spend Eternity. Our God is the alpha and the omega – the beginning and the end. His Kingdom lasts from everlasting to everlasting a very long time"

David was left to ponder all that Pastor Hussein had said. There was much study ahead, but he had the time. Amir had not yet returned from Israel with news from his parents. I sure hope I can go home soon thought David. This is all so confusing. However Pastor Hussein had all these charts showing what the Old Testament prophets had said thousands of years ago, and they are all obviously happening right now in my life time. How can I argue with all of this overwhelming evidence even our Rabbis are saying our Messiah should have come by now, howis it he has not arrived yet, except this fraud the Nazarene! That's just it, maybe He wasn't a fraud. Maybe this Jesus is our Messiah after all, just as millions of visitors who come to our country year after year believe.

Chapter 17

"David where are you son?" shouted Josh as he got to the phone on the first ring. "I'm in Enot Zugim at the Kibbutz Inn Dad"

"Ok stay there. I am coming to get you myself"

"Thank God" said Ruth. Then she started to cry with relief. "I want to go with you. I want to see my son!"

"No Ruth, it is best if you stay here. I can only worry about one of you at a time. I would be happier if you stayed here. Then I know you will be safe"

"I would like to go with you Dad" said Gershom quietly.

"Ok son, let's go. Let's go and bring your brother home"

Meara laid her hand on Gershom's arm. Gershom turned, looked straight into Meara's lovely dark eyes and said, "Don't worry, we will be fine" He hugged Meara and his mother, followed Josh, who was impatient to be on his way.

Josh drove quickly, confidently, but had obviously been thinking.

"I noticed yourself and Meara" said Josh hesitantly. "Is this relationship becoming serious?"

"Yes Dad, I have fallen in love with her. I want to spend the rest of my life with her"

"Hmmm" said Josh, "and Meara, how does she feel about you?"

"Well, I'm not too sure about that. I know she likes me, we have fun together. I can't rush her, so I haven't told her how I feel yet. Its early days, but I know how I feel, I'm quite sure she is the girl for me"

"Hmmm" said Josh once more. "Why did you have to go and fall for a Muslim girl? Are there no nice Jewish girls you could have fallen in love with. What is your mother going to say about this, eh?"

Well I'm not sure. Knowing Mum, I'm sure she suspects already, she seems to know everything about everyone without anyone telling her anything. Apart from that, Meara is a Christian, she is not a Muslim"

"Good grief, a what? A Christian!"

"You heard right Dad, a Christian"

"Oh no, I don't know what is worse. They are causing havoc amongst our young folk right now. They call themselves Messianic Jews. Messianic Jews indeed! There is no such thing. Shower of hippies if you ask me, they dance and sing on the beaches, encourage our kids to join them. They get baptized in the sea. Where is all this going to end?"

"Had I known this was going to be your reaction, I would never have mentioned the subject. You talk about antisemitism, peoples prejudice towards the Jews. You are as bad as they are. Your mind is made up please do not confuse me with the facts. Have you ever talked to a devout Christian? Do you actually know any Christians? Can you tell me what they think, what they believe?"

"Ok, Ok I get your point. I am listening. I am aware that we would probably not be coming to meet your brother had Meara been a Muslim. She would not have chosen to come here to stay in our headquarters flat in Jerusalem, certainly not the Jewish sector.

You are too young to remember what it was like in Palestine just after the Second World War. All the so called Christian countries like Nazi Germany hated the Jews and wanted to wipe us out. I escaped from Poland where every member of my family had been massacred. It was a very difficult time to be a Jew. You have read the history books, we Jews have been hounded and blamed for every calamity, in every country. It is still the same today. Russia is disintegrating at the seams who are they blaming as usual, 'The Jews' Hitler moved, invaded Austria, Czechoslovakia, France, Belgium, who intervened or tried to stop him? No-one tried to stop him not one of your Christian countries. Many of the Jews fled to Poland, but Poland would not allow them into the country. They were sent back, or to the gas chambers, concentration camps, or simply died from exhaustion, freezing cold winters, hunger, no one cared. When Hitler realized the other nations couldn't care less what happened to the Jews, he realized he could carry on with his wholesale slaughter of them unhindered"

"Gershom heard the anguish, the bitterness and the pain in his father's voice as he spoke. His father had never shared any of this before. "Why didn't they let the refugees come to Israel? Or Palestine as it was then"

"The British held the Palestinian mandate when they routed the Turks in 1917. They had promised us a homeland of our own through The Balfour Declaration. We had fought alongside them against the Germans in two World Wars, but they broke their promises time after time. It was The British who called the area Palestine after the First World War, though the Romans gave our land to our sworn enemies the Philistines after they destroyed our nation in 70 AD. The Romans called our land of Israel, Philistia Asteris. They knew that was the final insult to what had been to them a very troublesome nation"

"It still doesn't answer my question though. Why wouldn't The British allow the refugees to come to Palestine?"

"The British were pro-Arab. At least (The Labour Government of Britain at that time were pro- Arab then as now.) Oil is the key to understanding Western politics in the Middle East. God gave us plenty of oranges but no oil. The irony of this whole sorry saga is Israel has now found trillions of cubic tons of both gas and oil off the coast of Haifa. At this moment in time we are building a pipeline all the way to Cyprus, through Greece, through the Southern coast of European countries, to give them a much cheaper source of power than the oil coming from Russia. As you can imagine the Russians are not best pleased at this huge source of revenue being cut off from them so they are now siding with our enemies. We have Syria in the North. Then we have Turkey and Iran over to the East, along with their proxies, Lebanon and Hezbollah, Gaza and Hamas. Libya, Ethiopia and Sudan will join with them. They are gearing up for war. But, we are no longer the beaten, battered poor down trodden, Jews of old. We have built our nation to be a strong military power with formidable weapons. Our Mossad is feared all over the world. No place is impregnable to our operatives who operate in deep undercover dangerous positions to protect our interests and keep our people safe.It was our Israeli undercover operatives who discovered Iraq and Iran's secret stash of nuclear weapons. We cannot allow them to develop nuclear weapons so our I.T. guys developed a STYX virus computer programme. It is a UBS computer pen drive virus that our scientists inserted into their computers. The virus was active and destructive but did not activate for a year. It then blew up the Iraqi nuclear reactor in Osirak. A number of Russian scientists died in these explosions, the others decided this was no longer a safe place to be so they hotfooted it quickly back to Russia. We are also keeping close tabs on the situation in Syria did you see the photograph of Assad of Syria along with Putin of Russia, and Erdogan of Turkey shaking hands together?Very friendly, we also took out the Syrian Al Kibar reactor, and we are being blamed for the explosions at Natanz uranium enrichment facility in Iran. We cannot allow them to have nuclear weapons that would annihilate our very small nation we must do our best to protect our people. We have our early warning system that will blow up a nuclear device in the country of origin, but of course it will be reported world-wide that we struck the first nuclear blow on an Arab nation. As always we are dammed if we do and dammed if we don't. However my job is still to keep our people safe"

"How did you manage to get to Israel (or Palestine as it was then) that must have been an impossible journey for you at that time"

"Oh man, that was one crazy dangerous time. We were

just an ordinary family, living in Poland. My father was a good man, a baker, up every morning at the crack of dawn working to provide for his family. My mother was a good old fashioned 'Jewish Mama' she loved her family they were her life. I had two older brothers Elias and Micah, then Ruth our sister. I was the youngest, the baby of the family. War broke out when I was 12. At the beginning it seemed so far away. The elders and the adults followed the news avidly, but we children were not allowed to listen to the radio. We were sent out to play, or more likely sent to finish our chores. Then of course Hitler invaded Poland. We were no match for the German Blitzkreig, or crack German panzer tank divisions. The Germans sent over their Heinkel bomber 177sand their Luftwaffe double engine planes. They reduced our cities to rubble, men women and children blown to bits, bodies thrown into the air, walls tumbling down like ninepins. People were screaming in terror, confusion, deafening noise everywhere. The children were sheltered in the synagogue, but the bombers scored a direct hit, and every child died in the blast. The German bombers had concentrated on the Jewish district of Poland. Then the tanks rolled in and finished the job"

"You escaped though how did you manage that?"

"I was downstairs in the Bakery when the first wave of bombing started. I heard the sirens, then the blasts, people screaming. I hid in a corner, terrified witless, with my hands covering my ears to drown out the noise. I was huddled into the only wall left standing. Then things went eerily quiet, I very slowly crept out, and was grabbed literally by the scruff of the neck, lifted off my feet by Nathaniel. He was a big burly tailor, with a loud gruff voice. He surely used to chase us when we got into all sorts of mischief. He and the other men gathered me and the other few children left still alive, not many of us, only 9 children. Only 9 children can you imagine what it was like Gershom?"

"No, I can't imagine how frightening that must have been. I have been to bomb sites, and treated victims of car bomb's many Israelis have lost lives, but nothing on the scale that you lived through. How did you get out of Poland?"

"All the men formed a line and passed us down into the sewers! They stank to high heaven. It was pitch black, freezing cold, and home to thousands of rats. We walked for miles and miles through the sewers, until we reached the countryside. Under cover of darkness, we crept out and stole what food we could find. We hid and slept during the day and marched at night. We evaded capture and eventually reached the docks. There we found a boat sailing for Palestine. We were packed on this pretty small boat and cramped together like sardines. Many people did not survive the journey, they died, and many like me didn't care whether we lived or died anyway. All the people we had loved were dead or had been taken to Auschwitz concentration camp. We became deck hands and eventually reached Palestine. Israel? Supposed to be a Land of milk and honey? Not for Jews at that time. The British would not allow us to dock anywhere along the coast. Anyone attempting to go ashore was shot on the spot. However, Israel has a long coastline, with some lovely beaches. The British could not patrol every inch of it, so the Haganah, the underground resistance movement, would watch for the patrols and send out the smaller fishing boats to bring the refugees in. It was very dangerous, but we were doomed anyway, so we chose to run the gauntlet of British ships, at least that way we had a chance of getting into the 'promised land'. Some of us survived many more of us didn't, so I had no great love for Christians then or now. Don't talk to me about this Nazarene being our Messiah his followers have murdered more Jews than all the Arab nations put together"

"Ok Dad, at least now I can understand how you feel, but the Jews weren't innocent of atrocity either. How about the Irgun, the breakaway resistance group, they murdered and raped innocent Arab women and children in their villages. These men were Jews whether we like to acknowledge them or not. We are ashamed of the atrocities they committed, so Gentiles, Christian or otherwise, do not have the monopoly on murder, rape, and pillage. Men and women who hate, who are brought up to hate, commit atrocities against other human beings.

Meara was telling me about many Christians who did try to speak out against what was happening to our people. They were placed in concentration camps along with the Jews or were shot. In Yad Vashem the holocaust memorial museum there is a section for Righteous Gentiles who did help the Jews escape to Israel and did hide thousands of Jews from the Nazi's. Meara told me she read a book about a college in Wales, where they all fasted for days and weeks on end before the United Nations voted for Jews to be given their own homeland. Many thousands of Christians around the world are praying for our nation today. Presidents of many Christian countries are supporting Israel right now. Consider America, they have moved their embassy to Jerusalem, as have a number of others. At the Feast of Tabernacles we are happy to join with all these thousands and thousands of

Christians who come to Jerusalem to celebrate the Feast with us. Things are different today from the days after the war"

"That surely is a long speech for you Gershom. I guess you have been giving all of this a great deal of thought"

"I suppose I have been forced to. I have simply been a bit bowled over the last few weeks. Meara hasn't had any formal education as we have had but she reads anything and everything, well almost. She knows our scriptures dad, many of them off by heart. She is explaining so very much to me. It's all so matter of fact, I can't disagree with any of it. That is why this is all such a huge shift for me. Tell you what dad she could take on most of our Rabbi's and give them a real run for their money. They could not disagree with her any more than I could. I consider myself a good Jew as well"

"So, are you telling me you have become one of those 'Messianic Jews' then? If so------"

"Hold on a minute dad, I didn't say that" interrupted Gershom. "I am just trying to clear up some misconceptions here. I haven't made any decisions yet about anything. When I was in Medical school you gave me some excellent advice. If I want to prove something is the truth then set out to disprove it, in that way I will know for myself what I think I believe or disbelieve.At the moment, I have given myself a project. To prove the Nazarene could not have been our Messiah. Meara is helping me to pour over our scriptures, reading other books, posing, asking questions. It's like a journey we are both going on. I need to be convinced for myself. It sure is a fascinating concept though, and one we Jews will have to consider, our young folks are fast becoming believers in Yeshua. The Christian countries may have been our enemies many years ago but right now they are our closest friends and supporters. We cannot stand against every Arab country on our own. We are smaller than Scotland in the UK. Only 6 million Jews live in Israel today. We need our Christian friends."

"Ok Gershom, I hear what you are saying. I will keep an open mind, I'm sure this will not be the only discussion we will have on this particular subject. We are nearly at the meeting point it will be great to see David again. I can't wait to see your Mum's face when she sees him"

Chapter 18

Enot----Zuqim

Joshua's car was just rounding the bend into the car park, when a young male came running full pelt towards them.

"Dad, Dad, it's me!" Josh, shut down the engine, jumped out of the car and engulfed his son in a gigantic bear hug. Then it was Gershom's turn. Amir stood to the side, enjoying this long overdue family reunion. Josh was not letting go of his son just yet, hardly believing he was safe and secure, home at last. As Josh was chatting to Amir, Gershom placed his arm round his little brother's shoulder. "Well you have grown a bit since we last saw you. You haven't half led us a merry dance, Mum has aged 10 years since you went walk about one afternoon coming home from school. Quite an adventure you have had to yourself, did you enjoy your trip?"

"Well you met Meara out of it, didn't you?" Replied David giving his brother a mischievous grin. "I can read between the lines, I'm not meshuggah (a little crazy!) you know"

"Come on you two, let's get you home. Your mum will have her nails bitten down to the quick. She wants to see you son, and won't be happy until she sees for herself you are safe, and as cheeky as ever

Amir, how can we ever thank you? Will you come to Jerusalem with us spend some time as our guest, stay as long as you wish.... join our celebration this evening, I know our whole family would like to share a heartfelt thank you for helping David to escape and allow him to come back home to us"

"It was no problem, MR Lieberman. It gave me a little excitement in my rather boring, humdrum, day to day business. David is a great guy, a son you can be proud of"

"Please Amir, I would love you to come home and meet the rest of the family. Doctor and Mrs Solomon will expect you as well, won't they?"

"Ok, I am persuaded, how can I possibly miss this party? I love parties.

"Right that's settled then. Let's go, I just want to go home" The drive home was uneventful, with David chattering all the way telling his dad and brother all the details, embellished a little, David loved telling stories. "Dad, do you know why I was kidnapped?"

"Yes we do, but I can't share all the details at the moment. However we have gathered a great deal of information from Meara and our own operatives in the area. Amir has gathered quite a bit of intelligence on the situation. There is a terrorist group who want to do a trade with us. They will trade young Joseph for two of their members. Once you are home safe and sound we will get Joseph home safely as soon as this can be arranged. His parents know the situation and I have promised I will bring him home safely"

"That is great news Dad. I have been really worried about him. Now I can enjoy all the fuss and Mums great cooking, my own bed. This is so good. I really have missed all of you"

A few hours later Josh's car entered the Yemin Moshe district of Jerusalem and began the ascent of the familiar road that led to the Lieberman home. As soon as the car ground to a halt David bounded up the stairs to see his mum, and was engulfed in another bear hug, and smothered with his mother's tears of joy, and relief. Everyone was talking at once. David caught sight of Meara, sitting quietly in the corner, with a contented smile at the happy reunion. Meara was rather awed by all these people, and their exuberant obvious affection and love for one another. However David could hardly contain his excitement, so Meara was also caught in a brotherly hug.

"Well, hi you. And what have you been up to since I last saw you? It's really good to see you again Meara, I missed you when you came home without me"

"It's wonderful here David, your family have been so kind, as have Doctor and Mrs Solomon, and their daughter Rebekah. It's like my life has only just begun since I came here. I love it. And I am going to go to college soon. It is so exciting. I'm looking forward to it very much"

"School exciting "Meara, you are definitely meshuggha" as David touched his head in a gesture that implied Meara was a little bit crazy, but it was all lighthearted, happy fun, as a family had been reunited again.

The celebration party that evening was full of joy. David was home, now life could get back to some sort of normality. Life however would never return back to normal as it had been before. Life was about to change in Israel forever.

****

SYRIAN BORDER

Simeon and Yacov lay still as church mice, not a sound as they listened to footsteps approaching them. The silence was eerie after the deafening noise of sirens and explosions. Simeon was also puzzled: the noise he heard was coming from the opposite direction to the tunnels they had just demolished. The guards couldn't have run past them, he would have heard them. Simeon knew time was running out they could only have minutes more. Then he heard the sound again, it was very faint, but it was there. Someone was moving closer. His hands were sweaty as they tightened round the rifle. He was perspiring buckets, the sweat trickling down his back. Every nerve ending was alert and he was poised like a coil, ready to spring. Then he heard it, the pre-arranged signal of their unit. They had made it, they were here. He returned the signal, the guys had reached them.

Judy Harriman was the medic in charge of the Kidon team (This is a Mossad very secret undercover special ops unit) Judy and the team were waiting on the signal from Simeon and Yacov. They knew Yacov was seriously injured therefore it was imperitive they got them back to base and given medical treatment as soon as possible. Moving with great stealth the team reached the two exhausted, injured operatives. They both received emergency intervention. Fresh water, pain relief, binding bleeding wounds as fast as possible, they only had minutes before the whole area would blow to kingdom come. The last thing Simeon remembered was being hoisted onto a sling before he passed out.

The Kidon team moved very swiftly and efficiently away from the danger area to the waiting jeeps. They reached the phantom 2 jet with not a minute to spare and were fast on their way back to Israel with their precious cargo.

"Wow would you look at that Whistled Avi Cohen. The sky is lit up for miles and miles around. Glad we got the guys out in time. How is Yacov doing Jude? Will he make it?"

"Yep, believe so. We got there just in time. Goodness only knows what the guys have brought back with them - nothing good for our health that is for sure. This will set their bio terrorist programme back for a while and will cause an international outcry. They cannot prove it was us though. Guess it doesn't take an Einstein to work that one out mind you. Do we care? Not a jot! Time to go home people"

Chapter 19

The party lasted well into the early hours of the following morning so everyone slept very late. Much wine had been consumed in the Lieberman house that evening and a great banquet of food had been polished off. An open door for guests seemed a revolving door for many hours as friends, neighbours and other family members came to see for themselves one of their sons who had been brought back safely from the enemy camp. It was a great success. Josh was particularly pleased at the success of Simeon and Yacov being brought safely home with 'the package' the "headache was worth it" he thought as he wakened up with the worst hangover imaginable.

"Good morning Gershom" growled Josh. "Where are you off to at this time in the morning? Oh my head, it is splitting, do you have any good remedies for the world's worst hangover?"

"Here you are dad a couple of temgesic should calm your headache down a bit" as Gershom grinned his head off. It was most unusual to see his dad with a beezer of a headache. Still, it isn't every day your youngest son is returned safely home from a potentially lethal situation. Many young sons had been kidnapped and had not returned home. That is why in Israel today families walk together in groups. Children are not allowed to venture far from home, they stay close to Fathers side, especially orthodox families. However none of this was uppermost on Gershom's mind this morning, he was simply looking forward to spending time with Meara and showing her some more sights of the city.

"I'm just going round to The Solomon's to meet Meara. She said she would like to go visit Yad Vashem today. She has read about the Holocaust museum but never had the chance to go, so that is where we are off to later today. We will eat out so tell Mum not to bother cooking anything for us to eat"

It was a beautiful glorious sunny day in Jerusalem that morning as Gershom and Meara rode a leisurely bus journey to Mount Herzl that would take them to Yad Vashem. They were able to use their 'Rav Kav' smart- cards which have your photo ID on the back and allow you to hop on and off buses and light rail with the greatest of ease everywhere in the city and beyond. They are also great for tourists visiting Israel as they can be used on any mode of transport and handy proof of identity when required. They are also yours for life and can be topped up with shekels as required.

Gershom had forgotten how quiet the grounds of Yad Vashem were. He had not been back to visit since his school days.He was unprepared for Meara's reaction to the images and photographs that were shown in the different areas. They walked along the 'avenue of the Righteous among the nations' This is a road which commemorates the many non-Jews or 'righteous gentiles' who risked their lives to save Jews from Hitler's solution. They then walked through the hall of remembrance. Here is a permanent display of photographs from the Nazi concentration camps. The underground children's memorial especially affected Meara. The room was very quiet and dark except for the myriad pinpricks of light shining like stars. Each 'star' represented the life of a child killed or who died in the gas chambers. It was a sobering thought that one quarter of all Jews who died in gas chambers were children. When Gershom turned to Meara he saw the tears falling, she could not stop the tears from falling at the senseless waste of precious children's lives. One account touched her very deeply. It was the true account of one ladies journey from the book:

"Heroes of Faith"

'When a train filled with a large transport of Jewish prisoners arrived at one of the Nazi killing centers, many Polish gentiles came out to watch the latest group as they were taken away. As the disoriented Jews were gathering their possessions to take with them into the camp, a Nazi officer in charge called out to the villagers nearby "Anything these Jews leave behind you may take for yourselves, because for sure they will not be coming back to collect them!"

Two Polish women who were standing nearby saw a woman towards the back of the group, wearing a large, heavy, expensive coat. Not waiting for someone else to take the coat before them, they ran to the Jewish woman and knocked her to the ground, grabbed her coat and scurried away.

Moving out of sight of the others, they quickly laid the coat down on the ground to divide the spoils of what was hiding inside. Rummaging through the pockets, they giddily discovered gold jewelry, silver candlesticks and other heirlooms. They were thrilled with their find, but as they lifted the coat again, it seemed heavier than it should. Upon further inspection, they found a secret pocket, and hidden inside the coat was.......a tiny baby girl!

Shocked at their discovery, one woman took pity and insisted to the other "I don't have any children, and I am too old to give birth now. You take the gold and silver and let me have the baby." The Polish woman took her new 'daughter' home to her delighted husband. They raised the Jewish girl as their own, treating her very well, but never telling her anything about her history. The girl excelled in her studies, became a doctor, working as a Pediatrician in a hospital in Poland.

When her 'mother' passed away many years later, a visitor came to pay her respects. An old woman invited herself in and said to the daughter, "I want you to know that the woman who passed away last week was not your real mother....." she then proceeded to tell her the whole story. She did not believe her at first, but the old woman insisted.

"When we found you, you were wearing a beautiful gold pendant with strange writing on it, which must be Hebrew.

I am sure that your mother kept the necklace. Go and see for your-self" Indeed, the woman went into her dead mother's jewelry box and found the necklace just as the elderly lady had described. She was shocked. It was hard to fathom that she had been of Jewish descent, but the proof was right there in her hand. As this was the only link to a previous life, she cherished the necklace. She had it enlarged to fit her neck and wore it every day, although she thought nothing more of her Jewish roots.

Sometime later, she went on holiday abroad and came across two Jewish boys standing on a main street, trying to interest Jewish passersby to wrap Teffilin on their arms (for males) or accept Shabbos candles to light on Friday afternoon (for females). Seizing the opportunity, she told them her entire story and showed them the necklace. The boys confirmed that it was a Jewish name on the necklace but did not know about her status. They recommended that she write a letter to their mentor, The Lubavitcher Rebbe, explaining everything. If anyone would know what to do it would be him.

She took their advice and sent off a letter that very same day. She received a speedy reply saying that it is clear from the facts that she is a Jewish girl and perhaps she would consider using her medical skills in Israel where talented pediatricians were needed. Her curiosity was piqued and she travelled to Israel where she consulted a Rabbinical court (Beit Din) who declared her Jewish. Soon she was accepted into a hospital to work, and eventually met her husband, and raised a family.

In August 2001, a terrorist blew up the Sbarro café in the centre of Jerusalem. The injured were rushed to the hospital where this woman worked. One patient was brought in, an elderly man in a state of shock. He was searching everywhere for his granddaughter who had been separated from him.

Asking how she could recognize her, the frantic grandfather gave a description of a gold necklace that she was wearing.

Eventually, they found her among the injured patients. At the sight of this necklace, the pediatrician froze. She turned to the old man and said, "Where did you buy this necklace?"

"You can't buy such a necklace," He responded, "I am a goldsmith and I made this necklace. Actually I made two identical pieces for each of my daughters. This is my granddaughter from one of them, and my other daughter did not survive the war"

And this is the story of how a Jewish girl, brutally torn away from her mother on a Nazi camp platform almost sixty years ago was reunited with her grandfather.

Meara gasped, turned to Gershom and cried on his shoulder. Gershom simply held Meara until she was ready to dry her tears, and smile at such a beautiful ending to a harrowing frightening, war torn situation. A grandfather finding not only was his granddaughter alive after a terrorist attack but finding his other long, long, lost granddaughter that he did not know had survived the horrors of world war two. She did not die in a gas chamber she was alive, had come back to Israel and found her grandfather. What joy bubbled up inside Meara She laughed, clapped her hands, and danced around in a couple of circles until she realized she was not completely alone.The other observers chuckled at the joy of the young couple. They of course could not care less. They had found each other.

Chapter 20

Mossad Headquarters

Josh arrived late at Mossad headquarters the following afternoon. As he entered his department members of his staff were busily engaged in their research but the ops room seemed ominously quiet, much quieter than normal thought Josh. Generally the room was a hive of activity, with a lot of good natured banter and debate amongst the staff. Something was wrong, Josh sensed it instantly. He scanned the eyes of each member of his team but everyone tried to avoid direct eye contact with him. They looked to the floor, shuffled papers, walked to the coffee machine. It was an oppressive silence.

"Okay.... What's happened? Ari...? What's going on?"

Ari was most reluctant to comment. "You are not going to like this one bit Josh""Well someone had better tell me what is going on I would like to know sometime this century thank you"

Eventually Ari managed to tell Josh that they had listened to 'humint' an electronic surveillance link and were pretty shocked at what they had heard.

"We listened to some pretty nasty double dealing deep stuff Josh you are not going to like. Have a listen for yourself"

Josh placed the headphones on and listened to the voice carefully. The guys heard his sharp intake of breath. He knew that voice very well. It was the American voice of Tom Baker, the U.S. Secretary of State.

The voice said "the deal is set up and running. Loose ends are being tied up as we speak. Steve Armstrong is meeting with the Chinese. I have just returned from a Club of Rome meeting with our partners in Europe. They will back us 100%. I can confirm that we will deliver Jerusalem into your hands within two years at the very most. We have delivered on Hebron: you now have 80% of that area as we promised. When we begin applying more pressure you will have ....the land for peace swap, exactly as we agreed"

"Excellent" responded a quiet Arab voice in English. "In that case there will be no further attacks on U.S. interests: there will be no problems providing you keep to the deal"

There were other details exchanged on the tape but Josh didn't hear them. He was stunned at the importance of the information he had heard with his own ears.

He spoke barely a whisper:"Who was the Arab Tom Baker was speaking to? I presume you have traced the call?"

'Yeah....it was sheik Omar Bashir Rahman" replied Aaron "He is the leader of one of the Hamas Islamic Fundamentalist groups. He operates between Oman and Yemen. "We are checking him out further" added Daniel.

"We are being sold out Josh.... You heard the tape for yourself. The leaders in America and Europe have promised the Arabs that Jerusalem and most of Israel will be delivered to the Arabs within a few years at the most"

"I cannot believe this" said Josh, "the Americans are our allies. They cannot do this to us. What other proof do you have?"

Reuben handed a transcript of the tape to Josh, which he scanned quickly.

"What does this mean, I haven't heard of this 'One World Order....or this 'Club of Rome', who are they?"

"We are not sure, it was sheer luck that one of our I.T. guys picked up this signal and was able to track it. The language used was an old Etruscan dialect, and code names. Different countries are involved however our guys are on it. It was the conversation in English we caught that sent shockwaves through all of us. These guys are not speaking for their own Government they seem to have a long term agenda out-with their own governments 'knowledge"

"Do we know which governments in particular?"

"We know some of them. The G7 nations for sure plus the US that means France, Germany, UK, Canada, Italy, Spain Portugal. They are as always pro- Arab. TURKEY says JERUSALEM belongs to them they want it back. They are supported by Iran Iraq and Syria plus Hamas Hezbollah etc.Russia is joining them because we are chopping their oil and gas revenue with our new pipeline thru Cyprus.At least we have been given some warning Josh, you can be sure we will have all our guys on this. We will uncover it we always do. Our intelligence guys are everywhere undercover"

At that precise moment Josh was tired, he felt and looked old. His team had never seen him look so dejected. He was always so positive and optimistic. They were used to fighting heavy odds. Then Josh gave himself a shake. Ari was right.They did have some warning, mischief was afoot they just needed to dig and delve find out exactly what this weird sect were up to.

"Our God always warns us" said Josh. "HE has given us this land. It is our God given birthright given centuries ago. We will fight and we will win!"

With those words a sense of relief and hope swept over the team.

Then Nathan came in with another transcript. "Listen to this guys.....we have uncovered evidence confirming that the American CIA have been dealing with Arab terrorists, the transcript clearly supports this. No doubt about it the Americans will force us to hand over land once the Arabs promise that they will not target American interests. Guess our enemies cannot defeat us in battle but they will gang up and try to destroy us without a shot being fired. They will destroy our country economically mind you this Covid 19 virus is doing a pretty good job at the moment"

"We are not done yet" said Josh with renewed determination. "You have all done a fantastic job, I am proud of you. We still have much ground to cover. A few hours ago we did not have this information.Now we do let's go to work and find out exactly who are the brains behind this secret organisation. We must find out all we can about this New World Order He or rather they will be hidden in deep cover, or else we would have known about this sooner. Another thought has just occurred to me. As you know two of my close friends arrived from the States and the UK, they were saying that their intelligence departments had been infiltrated. That was why Andrew and Gordon flew all the way here to talk in person. This is all much deeper than we have been aware of. Right guys let's get to it! Uncover what you can and I will find out as much intelligence as I can from this end. Meantime though I have to get a move on I promised Ruth I would join her at Ben and Julia Solomon's tonight for a sort of welcome home celebration for David. Let's sleep on this and meet tomorrow 08 00 hours. Catch up for debrief then.

Chapter 21

During the worrying time David had been held captive in the Arab village, Ruth had become good friends with Ben and Julia Solomon, thanks to their introduction through Meara's friendship with Gershom. The Solomon family had made themselves freely available in supporting Ruth and Gershom during their time of worry. This support was greatly appreciated by Ruth in particular, primarily because Josh had spent most of his waking moments at work trying to resolve the situation. Julia had prepared a lavish celebration meal to celebrate David's safe return. The party was in full swing by the time Josh arrived. His late arrival was greeted with a loud good natured cheer. Julia handed Josh a plate to help himself to the buffet laid out on the table.

Having selected some delectable food he sat next to Ruth. He merely toyed with the food on his plate though. He was finding it really difficult to be sociable. Josh tried very hard to be light and jovial and to enter into the party spirit, but it just wasn't working. Before long it became very obvious that something was troubling him. Gershom was first to comment "Dad what's wrong?.... Is there something troubling you?"

Josh shook his head, "No, nothing, just some problems relating to workRuth knew Josh well enough to know that this was something more than a normal work related problem. "What is wrong Josh, you can share it with us we can be trusted. Whatever it is we will cope with it together"

Josh looked around the room at each member of his family he loved them more than they would ever know. He emitted a long weary sigh, he couldn't reveal too much, but this was family and close trusted friends he had to tell them something. Josh thought for a moment then decided to share some of what was concerning him. He told them he thought Israel was about to be betrayed and divided by their supposed allies. A shocked response swept through the group. Of all the people gathered in the room it was David who shocked Josh.

"Dad, pastor Hussein told me that things like this were going to happen. I didn't believe him at first. I honestly thought he was talking rubbish" After making this statement David sat back highly embarrassed, wishing he hadn't said anything. Every eye looked at him in astonishment.

It was Ben Solomon who was the first person to break the awkward silence as he encouraged David, "Tell your Dad David he needs to know"

David looked at Ben. "You know too don't you?"Ben Solomon simply urged "Tell your dad what you know and I will fill in the blanks. I believe we have a lot of information to share with him. Once we explain, perhaps what's now happening will make sense, that is, if you are ready to hear us?"

"What on earth are you talking about?" asked a very confused Josh. His news obviously wasn't the earth shattering bombshell to David or Ben Solomon that it had been to him.

"David began to share what he had learned from Pastor Hussein. Filled him in on some of the books he had read. What the Scriptures had said"

"Oh no" exclaimed Aaron, "not you too, what's happening, are all of my family being brainwashed?"

"Listen to him Josh, hear him out. Then pass judgement" urged Ben

"Alright just don't expect me to go along with all this nonsense" Warned Josh clearly upset by this unexpected turn of events. Ruth simply sat thoroughly confused by all that had been said. "Well I want to know what you are all talking about" she declared determinedly. "I seem to be the only person in the room who hasn't heard any of this before, so David, let me in on the secret"

David looked at his father and took a deep breath. "In the Christian scriptures, especially at the end of the book, it talks about events that will happen in our world sometime in the future. It especially talks about the things that will happen in Israel" stated David. "It tells us what will happen in many of the Nations not just ours though" The old Testament prophets Isaiah and Jeremiah also tell us what will happen near the end of time, especially the book of Daniel. It gives us the clearest timeline, and information as to what is going to happen on our planet. I have never heard any of our Rabbis explain the scriptures as clearly as Pastor Hussein did to me. He showed me in the book of Daniel where it states that in the final days a very evil man will arise out of Europe as a result of The treaty of Rome"

"Run that by me again David? Did you say Rome? Does it say that in the scriptures, our scriptures?"

"Yes" replied David a bit taken aback by his father's reaction.

"What else does it say? Tell me quickly" demanded Josh.

"They tell of an evil man called the antichrist who is going to deceive the whole world. He will at first appear like a great man of peace, who will bring order out of chaos. He will even allow our people to build a new temple here in Jerusalem. All the people will revere him as a great leader everyone will trust him. He will do away with money and we will have a card system only, but this will have a special mark. Everyone must accept this mark otherwise they will not be able to buy or sell anything......"

"Hold it right there. Slow down, explain this slowly to me. I need to see this with my own eyes" exclaimed Josh, looking straight at Ben Solomon who replied "You only have to ask Josh, I am happy to show you where to find all this information"

Ben went to his bookcase and removed a Bible from the shelf. The entire group had cleared the table and gathered seats around for this particular topic of conversation. Josh felt uncomfortable at the idea of a Christian Bible being opened here and being asked to read from the pages, however this information was way too important to be ignored if there was any truth in it. He knew he wanted answers to this club of Rome question. Every possibility had to be examined.

Ruth had sat quietly, until now she decided that she too wanted some answers. "David said something about a mark. What kind of a mark are you talking about, is it a tattoo of some sort, what will this mark look like?" asked Ruth more confused than ever.

"According to the scriptures the mark will be the number

666. You won't be able to see it. It is likely to be a miniscule microchip of some sort with all of your personal information contained on it. They will insert it into you index finger or thumb, and the powers that be will know everything there is to know about you. Track and trace will be in operation. Much like rich people get their dogs and children chipped so they will be easily traced if abducted. Possibly similar to electronic tagging so they know where you are every second of every day. Without this mark you cannot EFT/POS. ELECTRONIC FUND TRANSFER at POINT of SALE. You cannot buy or sell anything, so you will starve if you do not agree to take their mark. We are slowly but surely gradually being forced into a CASHLESS SOCIETY. Money will no longer be in use, banks will no longer be required. Every transaction will be done by computer really neat if you don't know the sinister motive behind it. Think about it, credit cards can be lost, stolen, broken, hacked and so on. To eliminate all of these problems each person will be offered the opportunity to have a microchip implant in their body, bible says either right hand or forehead. I personally reckon it will be our forehead, a person can lose their hand in an accident however if you lose your head I guess it will not matter too much. The idea is that once the chip is implanted, every time you make a purchase your chip or mark will scan and a direct debit will automatically record. I expect people would get a mite suspicious if you went to a checkout with someone else's head under your arm

Meara couldn't help giggling at this statement, quickly joined by Rebekah. Soon they were all laughing at the thought of someone trying to transact a purchase with someone's head under their arm. The laughter lightened the tension in the room, for a short time at least.

Josh asked the question "what has this to do with the 666 you mentioned."

"Apologies Josh I forgot to explain that part" Opening his bible Ben turned to the book of Revelation. 'Quite simply this mark is mentioned in Revelation chapter 13 v 15. Quote,

"He the antichrist required everyone both, great and small, rich and poor, slave and free to be marked with an inscription on their right hand or forehead so that no-one will have the power to buy or sell unless he has the mark. The mark is a human number 666"

"Are you saying this was all written in your bible 2000 years ago?"

"Yes it was here….. Read it for yourself. I think the mark may not personally be the actual number 666. It may simply be a combination of three sixes. Let me give you an example, each person can be identified by three sets of six numbers" Ben produced a writing pad and began writing as he spoke. "My date of birth is 19th May 1950. Therefore the first six numbers could be written 19/05/50

"Thousands of people share that same birth date" interjected Josh

"Absolutely correct" agreed Ben. Please bear with me thats exactly why there are three sets of numbers. Everyone has a national identity Number once you remove the prefix letters it leaves six numbers. Add those numbers to your postal Address or map reference, this also consists of three numbers latitude and three numbers longitude, yet another six numbers" Ben showed the piece of paper to reinforce his theory. He had written......

Date of Birth 19/05/50=6

ID Number 756432 =6

Map reference 321625 =6

"Each line comprises six numbers which could translate to 666. Those combinations will be unique to each person the information can then be inserted onto a chip and 'hey presto' you are chipped everything you buy can be direct debited from your bank account. In fact every move you make can then be traced"

"I'm sorry... I can't accept this.... It's an interesting theory but quite preposterous" insisted Josh.

"Fair enough" responded Ben posing another question. "Can you tell me if any of the information you use has been collected via satellite?"

"Yes I expect so probably the largest majority of it though I can't say for certain I'd need to ask Reuben about that. Why? How is this important?"

"My business is communications, FIBRE OPTICS. As you know I travel the world advising on communication cable links to different parts of the globe. I was in Japan recently organizing a network of FIBRE optic satellite cable links. This facility is capable of transmitting trading information instantaneously around the world. This is achieved by computers standing by to assess and interpret information in mere micro seconds. That's how quickly the transfer of information and banking transactions take place these days. On a simpler scale consider a satellite link up for the Olympic Games or world cup football. Pictures are beamed live to televisions in every country, in their own language all at the same moment, live as it happens"

"Yes.... I get that, so what are you saying exactly?"

"Over the last few years the world has become a global village thanks to computers and FIBRE-optics" said Ben. "Let me explain simply. Fibre optics are made up of microscopic filaments of dense FIBRE which are amazing conductors of light - more important than that they are capable of transmitting up to one 'trillion' pieces of information per second ONE TRILLION PIECES OF INFORMATION PER SECOND.

Whew! That's pretty impressive!" agreed Josh, "One trillion pieces of information per second.... But what has this to do with this mark?"

"I'm coming to that. There is a computer in Luxembourg, they call it 'THE BEAST' It contains information known about every single person in Europe, not only that, I suspect about everyone in this room. Information about each one of us can be placed on to a microscopic dot which could be inserted under every individual's skin. With the chip in place every time you pass through a scanner, much like an airport scanner, information will be automatically recorded. If need be every move you make could be recorded.'

'Rubbish! This could never happen!' responded Josh.

'Ben smiled, 'This type of thing is happening already! The programme began with inserting chips in dogs. The wealthy even have microchips inserted into their children's bodies. In event of a kidnap they can be easily traced. Certain types of criminal have chips inserted to keep track of them. The public have unwittingly accepted this first step. Simplest thing in the world is to progress further and inject everyone with a chip. Remember they only need three pieces of information to do this to every individual. Date of Birth, ID, and your address. Ben waited a few seconds before continuing. 'Think about it, three sets of figures arranged in a combination of sixes, or simply 666. Without this ID no one will be able to buy or sell anything. You can be traced anywhere in the world in seconds, amend that to micro seconds. There will be no hiding place....... no escape anywhere"

"Let me get this straight. You think that the head of this 'conspiracy' is a guy called the 'antichrist' He is working behind the scenes to take over every country, not just Israel. You reckon this is happening all over the world right now. You also think that a microchip plant programme will happen soon. When the plan is complete this antichrist will identify himself.....Is this what you are saying? Have I got that right?" asked Josh.

"Yes, that's about it.....however there is more" replied Ben. 'Other events must happen before the antichrist can be revealed.

"Like what?" demanded a frustrated Josh, "what more can possibly happen before this all takes place?"

"It's all going to be centred here in Israel" replied Ben. "The battle is on for our city of Jerusalem. Scripture records that all the nations are going to desert Israel. We will be left standing utterly alone. Not one nation in the whole wide world will support us, or come to our aid when the final battle begins"

Realization of fact was beginning to dawn on Josh. He wanted to dismiss the weight of evidence that had been offered. Perhaps he had been bound in Jewish tradition or he was simply too proud to accept the truth. He responded, "I can't believe or accept any of this, what evidence do you have? Can you show me exactly where you get this information?"

"I can" replied Ben "I will show you and explain to you exactly what is written in the scriptures and the Christian bible. Are you prepared for this Josh?" questioned Ben "Do you really want to find the truth?"

"I have little choice" replied Josh reluctantly. He felt uneasy at the prospect of his world being turned upside down. "I don't like this one little bit. Normally I would say you were all nuts into conspiracy theories, ready for the funny farm. I'm still not convinced that this isn't something from a science fiction book or an over active imagination"

Ben opened up his bible, as he flicked through the pages of the Old Testament he said, "These are the scriptures we were taught as boys Josh: the books of Isaiah Ezekiel Daniel Jeremiah Joel Zechariah etc. Josh nodded reluctantly in agreement. "Ben began his explanation. It was going to be a long night with much debate raging back and forth for many hours.

Chapter 22

By lunch time the following day Josh Lieberman was a very tired confused and troubled man when he met Gordon and Andrew as previously arranged at Fink's bar. They acknowledged each other with a wave and a nod of the head. Gordon noticed the frustration on Josh's face. "Had a bad night?" he questioned.

"Yes, you would not believe the lunatic discussion I had last night with members of my family - my own FAMILY!" said Josh emphatically smacking his hand on the bar in frustration.

"Do you guys know anything about a One World Order, a Club of Rome, and someone called the antichrist? Ben Solomon reckons that some conspiracy is being worked out right now; all the strings being pulled by some master conspirator. He thinks that this one guy is behind a whole crazy series of events" In an effort to calm his friend, Gordon replied. "I always work better with a cup of strong black coffee. Here, have a mug of the best coffee. I don't know much about antichrist but I do know something about 'the deep state' now calm down a bit, a favourite saying of my Dad was 'anger blows out the lamp of human intelligence' what you have just said makes more sense to me this morning and why I am here"

"Huh, I don't suppose your father was a messianic Jew by any chance" replied Josh with ill -concealed grumpy humour.

"No he isn't" replied Gordon with maddening calm "however he is an avowed Zionist"

"A Zionist, but he isn't a Jew! Now I've heard everything! What other revelations are you going to hit me with next? Forget all this nonsense... what's the latest news from Brannigan?"

Gordon smiled, "well the Syrians, and Iranians are not terribly enamoured with your boys blowing their underground nerve centre to kingdom come. Brannigan wired me a short time ago saying the American high altitude surveillance satellite has picked up a lot of arms movement. Brannigan reckons the Iranians are planning some form of retaliation. He's usually......."

At that moment an alarm sounded cutting Gordon off in mid-sentence. "What in tarnation is that infernal noise?" The men sprang from their chairs as if electrocuted. "It's an air raid warning!" declared Josh. "Quick follow me, no time for questions" Josh bolted from the bar with Gordon and Andrew hot on his heels. They didn't know exactly what was going on but they sensed the urgency of Josh's rapid departure from the bar, so followed his lead.

The sound was deafening. The harsh shrill of the siren struck alarm and terror into every heart. There was a sense of organized urgency with people being directed into purpose built air raid shelters. The three men entered a shelter. Andrew's heart was thumping in his chest. He breathed rapidly swallowing hard he looked around noticing that he was the youngest male present. The fear emanating from each person in the shelter was tangible, you felt you could almost stretch out your hand and touch it. With everyone safely inside the shelter, the steel bomb proof doors were closed and an emergency generator burst into life, the main lighting was shut down and replaced by softer light from red lamps. Gordon and Josh peered round the dimly lit shelter. They eventually saw Andrew and made their way over and sat beside him.

"At least we won't starve, not for a while anyway" commented Gordon. "There is plenty of food and medical supplies in here. Wonder what this alarm is all about? What's going on?"

"Quiet please everyone" pleaded Josh who was trying to listen to a newly installed radio system that linked all the shelters within the city of Jerusalem. "The report states that so far, three missiles have been launched on Israel. One at DIMONA, one at EN-GEDI and another at EN-HEMED, we don't have any reports on the nature of missiles just yet. It looks like our friend's the Syrians and Hezbollah have decided to cause us some bother with Iranian stockpiled missiles. I am awaiting further instructions so all we can do is sit tight until we get further information and the all clear through"

The wait was long and tedious, conversation muted. Andrew picked up his notebook and made copious notes and observations. He would write his story first hand and perhaps even earn some brownie points with his news chief. As he wrote, he thought, "Hope I stay alive long enough to deliver the whole story in person" The people who were gathered in the shelter amazed Andrew, they had to live with this type of threat every day of their lives. As Andrew interviewed them he learned from his fellow inmates that Israeli children were sent to school on different buses, because school buses are often singled out for terrorist attacks. Even inside the classrooms teachers carry automatic weapons to protect themselves and the children in their care. People living in the South of the country are aware that tunnels have been dugunder their communities, but the patrols who are ever alert, along with the latest weapons technology have so far been able to locate them and fill them in with tons and tons of concrete. It would be most unfortunate for individuals who may have been thinking up some mischief to get caught when an avalanche of concrete was coming their way. Many of the tunnels are very long, very wide and very deep, deep enough to take trucks and weapons through them sometimes for two or three miles at a single stretch.

Israeli's must be ever vigilant checking cars for booby traps, the police carry weapons; this is the price many are prepared to pay to live in their own land, indeed with the rise in antisemitism abroad many Jews are making Aliyah to live in Israel.

Forty minutes after the initial air raid warning had sounded the radio in the shelter crackled into life again. Josh listened intently then relayed the information to the occupants of the sealed shelter. "Thank God none of the missiles appear to have landed in any of our major cities. As far as we know sixteen missiles in total were launched against us" said Josh. "EN-GEDI appears to have sustained the worst damage. EN-HEMED was hit by four missiles and DIMONA two. Reports suggest EN GEDI has been almost destroyed. The emergency services are being mobilized as we speak. We should be given the all clear shortly, meanwhile we require volunteers. We require blood donors. Are there any medical doctors or nurses amongst us?" Several people responded to this call to duty.

Eventually the air tight doors opened and the people streamed out of the shelter in an orderly fashion. Andrew observed their reactions as they surfaced - they were becoming angry. Many were wondering if members of their family were injured or been killed.

Everything looked exactly the same as it did before the alarm sounded, but everyone knew things had changed - life would never be the same again. Volunteers were quickly organized into teams and efficiently dispatched to designated areas. Josh looked at both Gordon and Andrew. 'What would you guys like to do? What would you guys like to do? Do you want to come with me to EN-GED? Reports suggest it has taken a battering. It will be bad, prepare for the worst!"

"We know, and we are with you" replied Gordon speaking also for Andrew.

Chapter 23

The fifty kilometer journey from Jerusalem to EN-GEDI had not taken long. As they neared their destination they were aware of a heavy military presence in the area and helicopters were flying to and fro. Approaching the town the group thought they had prepared themselves for what they would encounter. Nothing in their previous experience had prepared them for the scene of devastation that met them as they entered what had been EN-GEDI. Not a single building had been left intact. Despite great activity there was a strange eerie silence broken only by the sound of rescue vehicles. As they entered the remains of the town, they could see soldiers and civilians searching for survivors who may have been buried alive. Dead bodies were lying in rows, many of the victims unrecognizable as human beings.

Andrew sat in the land rover rooted to the back seat in shock unable to take in the scene of carnage in front of him. He had never seen anything like it, he had covered war torn areas before but had witnessed nothing like this. As he sat in stupor he felt someone pull his arm. 'Snap out of it man! People are trapped under those buildings they need our help.' Andrew shook his head and without question turned and followed the member of the rescue team.

"What do you want me to do?" asked Andrew still in a state of shock. The soldier didn't answer instead he called out to the military nurse, "Judy another pair of hands for you" the young nurse seemed to be carrying out a dozen different tasks at once. "Put this on and follow me" she said brusquely passing Andrew a pair of orange coloured coveralls. Moving towards a group of people busily administering first aid the nurse asked? "Do you have any first aid knowledge?" Andrew hesitated, "only basic………""That'll do……better than nothing" exclaimed the nurse. "You can assist the triage team, as you can see we have limited resources, therefore we PRIORITISE and CATEGORISE casualties in order to maximize the greatest number of survivors"

Judy continued, "You will be looking for people with red tags meaning they require immediate attention. Blue tags mean injured but can wait for treatment. Black tags mean no treatment…. They are dead. I check the casualties over and say whether they can be lifted to the clearing station Judy called to another young man dressed in an orange overall. "Joseph, over here …. This is Andrew, he will help you to move the injured over to the clearing station"

Joseph was an 18 year old conscript. Both he and Andrew worked well as a team, each seeming to know and anticipate as through some form of telepathy what the other required. Hardly a word was spoken between the two men despite the fact Joseph spoke excellent English.

The first aid clearing station was situated on the edge of the town and close to the Dead Sea. The station itself was like a battlefield with dead bodies laid in neat rows ready for burial. Medics and First aid teams were desperately trying to save and repair shattered limbs and bodies. Speed was of the essence. A blood bank was quickly set up rescuers donated blood when they managed to grab a well-earned break. Whilst most of the rescue teams carried tags the medics had no idea of the blood groups of the injured, they simply prayed that the transfusions they were giving were rhesus negative blood and so compatible and a safe cross match. The rescue teams labored throughout the long hot day and into a long cold night with little time for rest. Thanks to their efforts many lives were saved.

Andrew looked around where he was standing, for a brief moment he felt as if he was staring down the scorched throat of a darkened tunnel into an abyss -so many people dead, injured, maimed for life '"What a tragic waste of human life" thought Andrew. His thought lasted only for a moment; time for philosophy later, right now there was still much work to be done.

Twenty two bone weary hours later too tired to think. Judy eventually announced, 'Okay folks, that's us done. Thank you for all your help we appreciate you all so much. Now time for bed, you have earned a long rest. Many lives were saved today, many husbands, wives children, parents will be returned to their families because of the hours you have put in today. Our casualties have been dispatched to various hospitals. Now look a helicopter has arrived with our relief team. Eat first then sleep for a week. I wish, you wish, no chance! See you next shift" Turning to Andrew the only non-military person in her team, she said a heartfelt thank you. "You were a great help believe me we appreciated your support. Do you need a lift can I drop you somewhere?"

"Thank you Judy, I appreciate the offer, but I will be returning with a couple of friends, providing I can find them. It's a frightful sight as far as the eye can see. All of these people dead. It's simply too hard to take in isn't it?"

"Yes" acknowledged Judy sadly turning to look at the shell of a community that had once been a thriving busy town. "These people have lost everything. Entire families wiped out, homes and businesses reduced to rubble. Will it never end?" She whispered quietly "we just wish to live in peace. Why can't they leave us alone? We have nowhere else to go"

"I don't know Judy. If it's any consolation not everyone is in agreement with what the Western politicians are doing. The majority of decent people want to help you to keep your land. We admire your sheer guts and determination for holding on to your land against impossible odds"

"Thanks Andrew, we do appreciate your support, the simple fact is - we have no choice in the matter. If we lay down our arms we die, I don't want another Masada, where we all agree to commit suicide rather than be taken prisoner. We also need strong support and your strong voice in the world press to give us a fair hearing. We need to let people know the truth of what is happening here"

"You can be sure I will do exactly that. I can't do what you do, but I am a journalist with UBC. You have my absolute promise I will use my influence to do what I can to get the truth out there" Judy appeared surprised at Andrew's statement, she responded not with words but with a hug and a kiss.

JERUSALEM

Thanks to Andrews contacts every major news-media corporation throughout the world provided extensive coverage of the attack that had destroyed three Israeli communities with great loss of life. The news reports added that the Israeli leaders and the people were outraged at the attack. The nation of Israel was in a state of shock and anger as they continued to clear up after the missile attack of the last 24 hours. The Syrians and Iranians knew to expect some form of retaliation, but where or when this would take place would be unknown until the attack happened.

Andrew discovered that the Jews were indeed made of sterner stuff. When he and Gordon met up with Josh they learned that the Jewish Intelligence network went quickly to work determined to find the locations from where the missiles had been launched. "What now Josh?"

"We will go into Iran and destroy their nuclear capability this time we must completely wreck their military programme. Hopefully we can do this with minimum loss of life. They should not have this facility anyway so I'm sure no one will mind if we remove it. It was our STYX programme that inserted the computer virus into their whole system.At deadly intervals their programme blew up destroying their system and the scientists at the same time. The Russian scientists knew they were being killed it was only a matter of time before it would be their turn, so they closed up shop and went home.

Within forty eight hours of the attack UN Peace Keeping Forces were being deployed into Israel in an effort to try and stop any further confrontation. The Middle East has always been a powder keg that could erupt at any time. Any level of reprisal attacks from the Israelis could easily and rapidly escalate into full scale war. The Israelis on the surface did not appear to retaliate immediately. Under the very noses of the UN they deployed

Special Service units with orders to destroy carefully selected Iranian military targets. The targets chosen were 'top secret.' as far as the UN were aware the selected targets did not exist. The sabotage missions were successful completely crippling the Iranian ability to launch any further attacks certainly in the immediate future. The Israeli attacks left the Iranians in a quandary. They could not claim that the Israelis had attacked their weapons sites. To have done so would have confirmed what most of the world had always suspected, that Iran was developing nuclear weapons in secret. This completely suited the Israelis. They had no need to admit or deny attacking Iranian sites. Even if they were suspected of retaliation the Israelis could logically conclude that they could not attack and destroy that which never officially existed.

Chapter 24

HADASSAH HOSPITAL

octor Gershom Lieberman was called to attend a patient in the Haematology Department of Hadassah hospital. The patient appeared to be a fit healthy young man of 24 years of age. He had been a victim of the bombing at DIMONA two days previously. Although he appeared uninjured he was admitted to a medical ward complaining of severe blinding headaches, raging fever, aches and pains throughout his whole body. His skin was jaundiced, paper thin and very tight. Gershom instructed the attending nurse to draw a blood sample from the patient and send it for analysis. As she placed a needle into the patient's vein, blood gushed out over the needle. "Looks like we have a bleeder here" she exclaimed as she tried to stem the flow of blood.

Gershom looked at the patients chart. "This guy is a regular blood donor there is no record of him being a 'bleeder" "This is very strange, Try again please" The nurse attempted to draw off blood and the same thing happened again. "His veins appear to be breaking apart as if he has haemophilia" she said.

"Set up a veinous infusion of plasma with Thrombo Kinase, that should help to clot the blood" Instructed Gershom more puzzled than ever.

"His blood pressure is still falling Doctor. It's falling

dangerously low" exclaimed the nurse with some alarm. To further complicate the situation the patient began to choke.

"Quick, pass me the laryngoscope please" requested Gershom as he tilted the patients head back in an attempt to keep his airway open. He attempted to pass the instrument down the patient's throat to see what could be causing the obstruction. As he did so black vomit bubbled up and around the scope. This was followed by vomit and blood spewing into the air. The projectile vital fluid of life and vomit showered the nurse and Gershom. The blood covered Gershom's face and ran into his eyes. Blood began pouring from the patients every orifice, from his eyes, nose, and ears. Great clots of blood fell on to the floor it could easily have been mistaken for lumps of spaghetti in tomato sauce. Gershom and the nurse could only stand helpless and horrified as the life drained out of the patient. He stopped breathing and died.

"What on earth happened?" pondered an astounded Gershom. "I've never seen anything like this before"

"Neither have I" responded Monique Bergman a senior nurse with many years of experience. Nurses are generally un-shockable however in this instance she was very shocked and upset by what she had just witnessed.

"What can it be? mused Gershom. "I don't like the look of this one little bit, collect some blood samples. "I will take them to the bacteriology lab personally" Gershom muttered more to himself than anyone else, "I hope Joel and or Fitz are still in the building" He turned to the nurse with very explicit instructions. "Before getting cleaned up, I want this area cordoned off tightly.

No one must be allowed to enter or touch this body. The fewer people who come in contact with whatever this might be the better" The nurse nodded in agreement as she handed him the phial containing a sample of the victim's blood that she had eventually managed to draw off.

Gershom quickly showered and changed into fresh hospital attire before making his way to the bacteriology lab. What kind of virus can cause this sort of destruction in so short a time? On reaching the laboratory Gershom was relieved to see Joel was still on duty. Joel was most surprised to see Gershom he noticed the worried expression on his face "what brings you here?" quipped Joel. Gershom went on to explain the circumstances surrounding his latest experience as he passed the phial containing the precious blood sample to Joel.

"Leave it with me, we will soon find out what it is. Meantime I would like to test a sample of your blood for contamination" said Joel. Gershom in his haste hadn't considered he himself may be at risk of infection from the blood that had covered him. "Better arrange to have Monique Bergman checked out. She was also covered in blood"

A few short hours later Joel called Gershom to the lab. He had part of the answer to the problem. "It is definitely a filo virus Gershom" reported Joel grimly.

"Uh huh and what's the good news" Queried Gershom as a cold shiver engulfed his body. Joel responded by shaking his head "there is none at the moment this is a new one to me. I've never seen anything like this before. I've called Fitz: he is on his way" He should be here shortly. Together we will work on it, all night if we have to" Joel looked straight into Gershom's eyes. "We have carried out checks on your own blood there is no sign of any infection. However I want to keep yourself and Monique in the isolation unit just to be on the safe side. We will observe you both closely for any infection. You need a few days rest and a good night's sleep anyway. How much sleep have you had these past few weeks"

"Not a lot now that you mention it. Normally Mum fusses too much but right now I think I would enjoy some of her fussing. Promise you will let me know the instant you find anything?" I want to know what we are dealing with here"

"Of course I will let you know as soon as we have anything to report. Now go home and let us get back to work"

Chapter 25

itz arrived at the lab shortly after Gershom had left and both he and Joel immediately got busy trying to solve what had happened to contaminate the blood of what appeared to be a healthy young man. Thanks to Fitz vast knowledge and experience it didn't take long to isolate the virus. "It is the Matreus Joel" I suspected as much from your description. The Syrians must have used a chemical filled warhead at DIMONA. 'Irresponsible fools' he declared angrily "we have got to be prepared for the worst. I have never known many people to survive this virus. It spreads like wildfire.....worse than the bubonic plague."

Joel looked at Fitz "Do you mean Gershom?" Fitz nodded "I'm sorry" he replied with regret in his voice. Shaking his head he added "I just don't see how he or the nurse could have escaped contamination, this is one of the most lethal airborne viruses known to man" Changing tone he continued "we had better alert the Public Health Department, looks like we are going to have an epidemic on our hands. People will soon be dropping like flies"

"What about an antidote?" pleaded Joel hoping and praying they would be able to use something against this lethal virus.

Fitz shook his head. "None so far, I know two of your Mossad lads did bring back samples of the virus, however we are not making any headway with a vaccine at the moment. Every time we come close the virus simply mutates into another form. It is a viral chameleon it can change to virtually any form making it impossible to track down"

"I promised Gershom I would let him know the minute I knew anything. I would prefer to go home and speak with him. What do you suggest we do?" enquired a dejected scared Joel.

Fitz heard the fear in Joel's voice. "I understand but you must be very careful - anyone who comes into contact is at risk. In the meantime we have to create an isolation unit where we can barrier nurse people who are infected with this. We will admit Gershom as soon as possible. We will require a very large sized unit. I will contact the chief medical officer and advise him of the situation and warn him to implement immediate medical and barrier nursing procedures. We have to try and isolate this infection as much as possible, try to contain the spread of the infection, although just how I don't know. Only an act of God can stop this Joel, better pray to the Almighty.....we need all the help we can get. We also have to place DIMONA and surrounding areas in complete lockdown to contain this bioterrorist attack. No one must go in or out. We will create an especially constructed isolation containment unit to isolate and treat those who are infected. We hit them with the cocktail of vaccines and drugs we knew were effective against the Corona and Mars virus. If we can quarantine the area quickly enough and folks go into complete lockdown soon enough and everyone prays very hard for Hashem to save our people once again then we may have a slim chance of surviving this horrific dastardly attack on our nation"

"That doesn't give me a lot of comfort right now. Thanks for all your hard work Fitz we appreciate it. I will get home and see how my big brother is first, then come back in and help you find an antidote for this pit virus that will kill many people world - wide. It is beyond me how any human being can be this irresponsible. However, if there is any way to beat this we must find it."

****

Josh and Ruth were both at home when Joel arrived in what looked like green overalls and carrying a case. Ruth took one look at her son and knew something was seriously wrong. "What is it Joel, what has happened?" she asked.

"I will tell you in a moment mom, I need to talk to Gershom first. Where is he?"

"In bed sleeping, he was exhausted when he came in earlier"

"Have you had any contact with him?"

Ruth shook her head. "No we were out when he came home. He left a note on the table asking us not to disturb him.......why? What's wrong?"

"Stay here mum, don't come into the bedroom. Gershom has been exposed to a highly infectious organism. All we know is it is airborne and highly contagious" Joel opened his case and removed breathing apparatus he slipped on the equipment before opening the door to Gershom's bedroom. He walked over to the bed and examined Gershom. He quickly exited the bedroom closing the door behind him. He instructed his father "phone the hospital. Ask for extension 5330. Tell Fitz we need that ambulance immediately!"

"What is it son? He doesn't seem to be that serious" pleaded Ruth hopefully.

Joel had made the connection. "It's this virus Joel isn't it?"

"Yes dad, I'm afraid so - that's why we must make arrangements immediately to get Gershom into the isolation unit as soon as possible"

Ruth of course had never heard of the Matreus virus so she had not a clue what the men in her family were talking about. "I will pack a bag and go to the hospital with Gershom" Ruth said quietly.

"I'm sorry mom you can't go to the hospital with Gershom"

"What do you mean I can't go to the hospital with Gershom, of course I must be there for him when he wakes"

"Dad".......Joel turned away, but not before she had seen the pain mirrored in his eyes and his efforts to stop himself crying.

"Josh" pleaded Ruth "what is happening, please tell me?"

"I will Ruth, I promise but first I must speak with Fitz at the hospital, give me a minute"

****

The ambulance arrived by the time Ruth had managed to pack a bag for Gershom. The paramedics entered the Lieberman house wearing similar green attire as Joel, they also wore breathing apparatus. Realization dawned on Ruth just how serious Gershom's condition was. Within minutes Gershom was in the ambulance accompanied by Joel and heading for hospital. Ruth and Josh stood at the window watching the ambulance with her two sons inside disappear into the night. Ruth remained gazing through tear stained eyes into the night sky for some time. "What can I do" she thought. She wandered in a daze around her spotless home, tidying and cleaning items that were already clean. "There must be something I can do..... pray.... what else was there? The Almighty gives life, only HE can give it or take it away. Josh on the other hand thought that work was the solution to Gershom's plight, find out more about this virus. He tried to reassure Ruth before he bade farewell and left for his office. Standing there alone the silence in the Lieberman home was unbearable. Ruth on impulse decided to visit the Solomon's. They were friends who had become close over the last few months.

Despite the lateness of the hour the Solomon's warmly welcomed Ruth into their home. It was obvious something was wrong. Within a short period of time Julia had extracted the news from Ruth. Both Julia and Ben expressed their support and immediately tried to comfort and reassure her. They talked of many things, of their children and of the terrible things that had been happening lately. Ruth was fraught with worry, "First David was kidnapped now Gershom has this illness...What next?Why is all this happening?"

"This is what we were trying to warn people about the other week.These things were written down in our scriptures many years ago to warn us these things will happen"

However this was of little concern to Ruth at this moment in time. Ruth was not the slightest bit concerned about any of those things. She was a mother and her son was seriously ill.

She understood that no one expected Gershom to survive she just needed someone to talk to.

****

Meara was wakened when she heard the voices in the downstairs living room. She slipped on her dressing gown and joined the Solomon's and Ruth downstairs. It was obvious something was wrong.... Something serious had happened. Ben Solomon looked at Meara, "Its Gershom he is in hospital" he said quietly. Meara didn't wait for a full explanation. The atmosphere in the room said that it was serious. She dressed quickly and made her way to the hospital. She was refused admittance to visit Gershom. In frustration she asked to speak to Joel. It was sometime before he could get away from the lab, but he finally arrived. "Meara what are you doing here?"

"I have come to help. Joel... Please don't send me away, I won't go" stated Meara with quiet determination. "I know something serious is happening and that you will need all the help you can get. I am not a nurse but I know how to look after people who are ill. I can help to care for Gershom. Jesus will heal him Joel I know HE will. HE can do what your medicine cannot do. Please let me stay. I am not leaving here you may as well put me to work. I know how serious this virus is, I want to stay" insisted a determined Meara.

"Whew....Meara, I don't know if this will be allowed. The rules are very strict in Quarantine" However Joel knew Gershom would want Meara to stay by his bedside. Everyone had noticed how both Meara and Gershom were besotted with one another. They had become very close over the last few weeks. Joel knew

Gershom loved this sweet beautiful lady, and she had obviously come to love Gershom in return, although his brother did not know it. It seemed that Gershom would never know of Meara's love for him as he had slipped into a coma. "This is so unfair why should this happen to a good man like Gershom?"

"Meara" said Joel holding both her hands gently "this is against every rule in the book, however if love can make a difference where medicine can't, then I will personally move Heaven and earth to let you stay with my brother. I love him too. I believe you can make a difference"

"Thank you Joel" said Meara her eyes glistening with unshed tears.

Meara was given a pair of green coveralls and shown to the room where Gershom lay in an 'air tight cylinder' and a life support machine breathing oxygen into his pulmonary system. She began her long vigil, sitting by Gershom's bed day and night. She moved only when medical staff came in to carry out care, tests or examinations. Gershom was one of the most popular young doctors in the hospital. Medical staff in their own hospital always looked after their own and of course it was imperative they found some sort of antidote that would be effective in the treatment of this lethal virus. Meara slept very little, hardly ate but she prayed oh how she prayed. "Dear Lord Jesus. You healed many people of every kind of physical, mental, emotional illness and disease when you walked through this land, perhaps on this very spot where I am sitting right now. I plead with you please touch Gershom with your healing power. You tell us we have not because we ask not. I love this wonderful man so much, only you have the power to stop this terrible virus from claiming

Gershom. Father God, help Joel and Fitz to find a vaccine to stop this evil virus from killing thousands of our people. You are The Mighty One of Israel, the Lion of the tribe of Judah. You promised to protect and keep your people. I am reminding you of your promise Father. You are a Covenant keeping God. Even when we are faithless YOU are faithful Thank you Father for hearing my prayer. In Jesus precious name I ask this. Amen"

For two days Gershom hung on to the slender thread of life as the virus continued to rage within his body, yet death seemed unable to claim him. Fitz and Joel tried every cocktail of drugs they could think of that could possibly help to combat this viral killer desperate to snuff the life out of this precious young man. One glimmer of hope remained Gershom was still alive he wasn't dead yet. "This is very strange" thought Fitz to himself. "What on earth is going on here - forty eight hours and no further deterioration this is unheard of. During the next twenty four hours the death rate from the virus began to rise. At first the casualties comprised mostly of hospital staff and people who had been in contact with victims of the DIMONA bombing. This confirmed what Fitz feared their enemies had stooped to a bio terrorist attack and detonated a germ warhead in DIMONA.

We had better make arrangements to incinerate every dead body and every particle of clothing connected to every person who dies of matreus" Fitz advised the relevant authorities for infectious diseases.

Throughout all of Israel prayers were said. Others searched the scriptures looking for clues and instructions God had given to Moses when he led the children of Israel through the desert and free from every disease if they would keep and follow Hashem's commandments. In the wilderness they were given instructions to build latrines outside the camp. Carry spades and shovels to cover excrement. Wash hands thoroughly in running water. Bathe regularly. Refrain from intimacy during a female's menstruation period. Do not eat certain foodstuffs. Some animals were safe to eat others were not. Any infectious disease for example, leprosy must be treated out-with the camp and the afflicted must not be admitted back into camp until they had been examined carefully and deemed to be free of infection. However this was a bio terrorist attack. A very lethal virus had been harvested in a human science laboratory. The DNA genetic code had been altered making it impossible to clone an antidote to the genome sequence. Finding one would be almost impossible. How and ever the Lord of the Universe, the Creator of the sun the moon and the stars and the planets will not be mocked nor will HE be surprised at the depravity of man towards his fellow human beings. HE alone could help the people of Israel now. The people prayed the scientist's virologist's epidemiologists and bacteriologists, lab technicians worked around the clock to crack the genetic code. Nothing worked. The virus continued to rage unabated throughout the land. People were constantly being admitted to the hospital dying from this contagion. The result was always the same, the victims died within a short space of time. Gershom however refused to die - he hung on tenaciously to life.

On the tenth day of Gershom's confinement came a sudden break through. Meara was dozing when she heard her name being whispered. "Meara is that you?" asked a very emaciated weak Gershom. "My throat... I'm parched. What happened?

Where am I?" Meara sat with tears of joy streaming down her face. "Gershom....I knew Jesus would heal you. You have been very ill, but now you will be well my love, light of my life, do not ever give me such a fright again"

Gershom did not hear her he had drifted off to sleep again, however this time it was a more natural sleep. Meara tore off down the corridor to share the good news with Ruth who was sleeping in the anti-room. "Ruth! Gershom has wakened!" He is going to be well! He is going to be fine!" Both women clung to each other laughing and crying at the same time. A nurse came to see what all the commotion was about. On hearing the good news she joined in the happy celebration. She realized the significance of Gershom's recovery. Gershom's blood would contain antibodies from which the bacteriologists could make an anti-viral serum. This was the major break thru that everyone had been hoping and praying for!

Meara returned to Gershom's room, slipping in quietly to say goodbye to him. As she entered the room he heard her and opened his eyes. He motioned to her to come closer. "Joel told me how long you have been here. Thank you" He paused. "I love you Meara very much. I would like to spend the rest of my life with you. Will you marry me?" adding "you can't say no..... my doctor said I mustn't be upset"

"Well now we can't have you being upset, can we? Of course I will marry you. In the meantime you must concentrate on getting well" smiled Meara. Gershom nodded and managed a cheeky grin. "Don't worry I will be up and about soon, then we can be together always"

"The most important thing right now, is rest. I must go now I promised that I would only stay a moment. I will be back soon, goodbye my love" Meara blew him a kiss as she left the room.

Chapter 26

Within a short space of time thanks to the antibodies taken from Gershom's blood sample, an anti-viral serum was able to be manufactured which had a positive effect. The death rate slowed and then started to decline. The countries had learned some lessons from the coronavirus virus only a few short years before. After another full week in hospital Gershom was champing at the bit to go home. He was feeling a great deal better and was in no mood to spend endless days in a hospital bed. His consultants knew that he would be very well looked after at home so they allowed him to leave hospital to continue his convalescence there. It was an open secret how Gershom and Meara felt about each other. They spent every waking moment together simply enjoying each other's company. They now had a different problem which would have to be addressed soon. Where would they be married?

****

Over the following weeks Gershom and Meara spent endless hours discussing spiritual things, especially with Ben and Julia Solomon. "I have become a believer Ben, I cannot deny I truly believe I would be dead today if yourselves Meara my family and other believers had not prayed and asked YESHUA to heal me. I now understand for myself" explained Gershom. "I accept all that the Holy Scriptures speak of regarding the times we are living in, the signs scripture points to what will happen next on Abba father's time clock. It both excites me and scares me at the same time. I very much enjoy the Bible studies you and Julia hold in your home here. I know Meara and I have many friends here........but, we just don't know what to do for the best. We don't want to hurt my parents. My mum is perfectly accepting whatever we choose, but you know how dad feels. He cannot accept in any way shape or form that Jesus is not only the Christian Messiah but is our Messiah too"

"Gershom you have a staunch ally in your mother" said Julia. "We hold a ladies meeting here every Wednesday morning and your mum has been coming along for several months now. She too has become a believer in YESHUA as her Messiah"

"My mother?!!! Coming along to a bible study here? Well that sure is a surprise she hasn't said anything to me about it" replied Gershom in astonishment. "Yes she started coming along when you were in hospital. We held a prayer vigil for you and all of Israel. We prayed around the clock in 2 hourly watches, your mum became good friends with the ladies in our group. She knew they cared for her and that everyone believed God would heal you Gershom. It helped her to hear others praying with utter conviction. They were in no doubt that YESHUA would raise you back to perfect health again. That is what our God does for our children Gershom He loves you more that we do. Now here you are living proof of our living God. Awesome isn't H?"'

"HE sure is" agreed Meara wholeheartedly.

"Well with mum on our side as well, we just need to convince dad. Why can't he see the truth? It is so obvious" cried Gershom in frustration.

"You must be patient with your father" said Ben. He is worried with a great deal to concern him at the moment. He has to make difficult decisions affecting millions of people's lives. He knows that Israel is in great danger and doesn't yet realize God Himself will protect our nation"

"I know replied Gershom. "I want my dad to give his blessing when I marry this amazing lady here" Gershom swung Meara around in a big circle he loved to hear her squeal with delight.

"Humm.... not much wrong with him" commented Julia with a smile to her husband. It was difficult not to be caught up in the young folk's excitement.

MOSSAD HEADQUARTERS

Mossad headquarters was its usual hive of activity. "What on earth is wrong with the chief?" Judy asked Andrew. "He sure is grumpy this weather. You would think he would be happy with the way things have turned out for Gershom"

"Well that is part of the problem. His son is getting married soon" replied Andrew.

"Who Gershom?" asked Judy in surprise.

"Yup.... That's the one"

"Why on earth should he have a problem with that? You would think he would be overjoyed that he was still alive to get married" stated Judy.

"Well the problem from what I can gather is his wife to be is an Arab lady and a Christian at that"

"What a Christian Arab? Oh I see Josh is worried that his son is marrying outside the Jewish orthodox custom, is that it?"

'"No, not exactly" replied Andrew slowly "it's rather more complicated than that. They are being married by a Jewish Rabbi in a synagogue"

"Hold on Andrew. Take this just a bit more slowly for me. I think I am missing something here. We have a Jew being married to an Arab Christian by a Rabbi in a Synagogue! Well that covers most of the bases I guess. Why does Josh have a problem with that?"

"Tell you what, why don't you have dinner with me tonight and I will do my best to explain what I think the problem might be"

"Mm... ok why not. Not one to miss an opportunity, are you?" teased Judy. She had grown fond of Andrew over the weeks they had worked together. Andrew was young, attractive, informative and fun. He had followed her instructions carefully without question during the missile attack. "Yes, ok it's a date, what time and where?" asked Judy.

"You will! That's wonderful....great...I mean.....yes right" Andrew just couldn't believe his luck. He had liked Judy from the first moment he had seen her. He found her extremely attractive (along with dozens of other guys of course.) He hadn't dared ask her out sure she would turn him down flat.

Chapter 27

"Josh I know you are tired and have a great deal on your mind" ventured Ruth. "However we do need to talk, you seem to have been avoiding me. There are things we need to discuss"

"Ruth, I know that, but must we talk about all this right now? I just need some peace and quiet to get my head around all of this"

"Yes we must, time is creeping up fast we have lots of decisions to make and a wedding to organize. It will not just disappear. Gershom and Meara want to get married, they love each other, and they will be married with or without your blessing. However it will mean so much to Gershom if he could have it you have been immersing yourself in work so that you do not have to think about this, but it is time Josh. We are family and we love you. Are you seriously going to allow religion to separate you from your family? This is all about relationship Josh not religion"

"It's all this Messianic Jewish nonsense I can't cope with" responded Josh irritably. "I don't believe it, and neither do you"

"When did we last have a conversation Josh?"

"What kind of a daft question is that? I speak to you all the time. I spoke to you yesterday, and the day before that, and the day before that. What are you saying to me woman?"

"If only you would take the time to listen, you would know

that I too have become a believer" declared Ruth quietly.Josh was stunned. He looked at Ruth, the woman he had loved and lived with for 38 years he just could not believe what she had just said.

"No Ruth, I don't believe you. How could you? When?" responded Josh in disbelief.

"Unlike you Josh, I decided to give this matter some thought. Julia and I have become good friends, to be honest I don't think I could have survived those terrible days when Gershom was lying in a coma and we were expecting him to die along with thousands of our friends and neighbours. Julia was there for me. This is not about religion Josh this is about a personal relationship with a loving Heavenly Father. He is not a distant omnipotent being who doesn't care what happens to us. HE cares about you and me about each one of us as individuals. Julia and her friends prayed for us as if we were their very own family. I wanted and needed the strength and the faith they had for myself:! Now I have it Josh. I now have a relationship with Hashem through YESHUA for myself"

Josh stared at this woman whom he loved. He thought he knew her, but she was different today. She spoke with a conviction he knew he could not change - not today or any other day. Josh felt such conflicting emotions course through him. His mind could not concentrate this was such a shock to him. He felt betrayed, that was it - he felt betrayed by the woman he loved and he had believed loved him.

"Gershom and Meara are getting married in a month's time at the Messianic Synagogue. Rabbi Cohen will conduct the marriage ceremony. Gershom has been trying to talk to you but you have been 'too busy' to spare the time, you are rushing around here there and everywhere busy with matters of 'State' with no time to talk with any of us. I do hope and pray you will take the time to come to your son's wedding. Forget religion Josh, find a relationship!" With that statement Ruth got up from her chair kissed Josh on the for-head and went to bed. Josh went over to the cabinet and poured himself a stiff drink. His mind was in a quandary too active for sleep. He decided to go to the office where he worked until he was too tired to think. He fell asleep at his desk.

****

The wedding preparations were well in hand as the big day drew near. As well as her many other talents Julia was a gifted seamstress, she had made a beautiful wedding gown for Meara. Ruth gasped when she saw Meara in her gown, "Meara you look absolutely beautiful" What a radiant bride you will be. Gershom is so fortunate to have found you.... of course David takes all the credit for this, he found you all by himself and brought you back home just for his big brother" The women laughed, very much at ease in each-others company. Ruth had indeed found the daughter she had always longed for, and Meara felt very much loved and accepted in Gershom's family. The two women laughed and enjoyed the fellowship and excitement of being involved making arrangements for the forthcoming wedding.

Gershom knocked on the door of the room where they were working. Opening the door slightly Ruth said, "you can't come in we are preparing Meara's wedding dress. You cannot see it until your wedding day"

'"It is the wedding I have come to talk to you about mom. I have been trying to speak to dad for weeks but he is never available. Do you think he will come to the wedding?" asked Gershom.

"Yes Gershom I am sure he will..... I will speak with him again. He comes home from the office late and leaves early the next morning. He obviously doesn't want to discuss anything, so I carry on as normal, waiting for him to talk. You know your dad he likes to think everything through in his mind first, only then will he make his decision"

"He refuses to take my calls when I call him at the office. They tell me he is away on business. What on earth can you do when someone totally refuses to speak with you?"

"Not a lot Gershom except wait. He loves you, you know that. He also cares for Meara. This has nothing to do with her. This is all about his personal journey of faith. We can only pray he comes to terms with the situation gets over himself and come to your wedding. I believe he will"

****

Life was frantic in the Solomon household as they prepared to make their way to the wedding venue. Meara had invited Rebekah to be her bridesmaid so the excitement was sky high as they were getting prepared. Meara could not quite believe this was all happening to her. She prayed to her Heavenly Father thanking HIM for all the wonderful things that were happening in her life now. She thanked Abba for her new family, and for Gershom, she just couldn't believe she was going to be married to this wonderful man in a few hours-time. She prayed that HE would bring Josh to the ceremony especially for Ruth and Gershom. She prayed the whole family could be united together on this very special day. Now the day was here, all they were required to do was get to the synagogue on time.

It was a beautiful day, as expected the sun was shining. Gershom's heart almost burst for joy when he saw his father arrive at the synagogue with Ruth. Gershom walked over to his dad hugged him and simply said "thank you for coming it means a great deal to Meara and I. We hope we will have as good and as strong a relationship as you and mum have had. David Joel and I have been very fortunate. We could not have wished for better parents. I love you dad, I just wanted to tell you that" Josh hugged his son. "I am very proud of you Gershom I wish you and Meara a lifetime of happiness" Gershom invited his father to sit with his mother as the ceremony was about to begin. Little did Josh know that was the last time he would ever see his son again. So often in the months ahead he would think back to that conversation and wish he had said the words that were in his heart that day. After the wedding ceremony Gershom and Meara had driven South to EILAT to stay in the beautiful King Solomon hotel to spend their honeymoon. That was where they were on that fateful day. Josh would never forget it was etched on his memory forever. He would never see his son again.

Chapter 28

It had become normal practice for Josh to arrive home in the early hours of the morning. He went quietly upstairs and looked into the bedroom, Ruth was sound asleep. He tiptoed quietly into the bedroom changed into his nightwear and slipped into the bed beside her. He soon fell sound asleep. Something wakened him in the middle of the night. It was still pitch dark. He switched on the bedside lamp and looked at his watch, 3.25am. He turned to Ruth she wasn't there. Her watch was lying on the pillow with the clasp still fastened. 'How did she get her watch off without loosening the clasp' he thought. He noticed that her night dress lay draped under the bedcover in the position that Ruth had been sleeping in. The gold necklace he had given her on her fiftieth birthday was also lying on the pillow still clasped. Ruth never removed that necklace, not even to shower. It was impossible to get this necklace off without releasing the safety catch. 'Strange' he thought. He called her name but got no reply. 'Where was she?' he thought, 'she will have gone to the bathroom' He got out of bed and knocked on the bathroom door expecting it to be locked. There must be a perfectly logical reason for this, surely?' The bathroom door swung open it was in darkness, the light was switched off. Ruth wasn't there either. "Ruth! Ruth!" He called, 'where could she be? It is the middle of the night. Josh switched on the house lights and searched every upstairs room. He went downstairs, still no sign of Ruth. He checked the front door it was locked from the inside his key was still in the lock where he had left it earlier.

As he continued his search the telephone rang, he picked up the receiver it was Joel phoning from the hospital. 'Dad... something very weird is going on here. I was in theatre waiting on some tissue samples when the surgeon who was operating on an emergency case disappeared in front of our eyes....he simply vanished.!! A number of other staff members vanished at exactly the same instant. One second they were there the next they were gone. They just disappeared like into thin air. The rest of us just stood looking at each other wondering what on earth was going on. We heard a commotion outside the theatre, some of us went to see what the disturbance was only to discover that many other people had disappeared too, all exactly at the same time as the theatre staff. Josh felt a deep dread in the pit of his stomach. His body went numb. He managed to mumble to his son that his mother seemed to have disappeared also.

Joel responded in shock. "What....mum has gone too? Dad is this it? Is it this Rapture thing that Mom, Gershom, David, Doctor and MRS Solomon were always talking about?"

"No Joel....it can't be. There must be some logical explanation for this. I will phone David, he is staying over at the Solomon's house tonight"

"I'm coming home Dad. I will be there shortly!" Joel rang off. Josh immediately tried to phone David at Ben and Julia's home. The phone rang out and Josh knew deep in his heart they had all gone. None of them had been left behind except himself and Joel. Josh was simply numb as he made his way across to the television. "That's it see if any of the news channels are saying anything BBC or CNN world news. Surely that will put an end to this nonsense" thought Josh desperately. He switched on the television and sat back, or rather fell back into his armchair in complete shock. On TV news reports were showing total carnage in many countries around the world. Live broadcasts from Washington included numerous reports of traffic chaos, with multiple pile-ups on all the motorways. The news reporter stated that driverless vehicles seemed to have caused the accidents. It was as if people had somehow mysteriously disappeared whilst driving on the highway. Josh flicked through the different TV channels. Similar reports continued, a number of aircraft had collided in mid- air, the pilots had simply disappeared from all accounts! Some airport controllers had also mysteriously disappeared. Driverless trains smashed into each other. "What on earth is going on?" thought Josh in total shock. I just cannot believe this is all happening but it's going on in front of my eyes. I am watching it happening in front of me! I cannot deny what I am seeing right now!

Similar experiences and news reels were being reported from every part of the globe, every country. People were vanishing into thin air. Primary schools, pre-schools, nurseries crèche and childminder facilities were left totally empty apart from one or two teachers staring at empty desks. Young children and babies simply disappeared. Mothers in maternity units were left literally holding the bottle as the baby they had been feeding was no longer there. Only some adolescents above the age of eleven were still present. What was going on? Everyone was asking the same question. Where had all of these millions of people in every country disappeared to? All sorts of theories were being muted. Being abducted by an alien race of strange beings was among one of the favourites. Josh knew better. He knew exactly where they had all gone. His arrogance and stubbornness had caused him to be left behind. The other immediate problem issues were staff shortages causing communication and computer systems to crash. Lack of staff caused problems with power, gas, electricity, wi-fi networks begin to fail. Mobile phones, e mails, social media will all pack in. Soon it will be panic buying food, how to cook the food. Milk, fresh water, sanitation, hospitals, none of this bears thinking about thought Josh. A stiff drink might help take the edge off this. Ruth would have withdrawal symptoms from lack of coffee. She liked her coffee strong and black. Josh was just beginning to comprehend the magnitude of this event, this Rapture that had taken place as Ruth had mentioned 'In the twinkling of an eye' she had called it.

Josh felt so very lonely at that moment. The people closest to his heart had gone. He placed his head on his hands and cried, wept like a child. He felt more despair and fear at that moment than he had ever felt in his entire life. This situation was even more terrifying than anything he had experienced in Warsaw when the Nazi's were bombing the city.

He lifted his head when he heard the key turn in the front door lock. He hoped against hope that it would be Ruth and he would awaken from this nightmare. He watched in vain anticipation as the door opened and a very frightened, shaken Joel walked into the room."Dad..!" Josh heard the fear in his son's voice. "What is happening?" What is going on? It's chaos out there. I had to walk from the hospital, it is impossible to drive on the roads just multiple pile-ups and crashed cars, vans, and trucks, everywhere total carnage. People are going crazy looking for their loved ones, calling and screaming out the names of people they are looking for. They are running around like scalded cats. The police and army are trying to gain some control. No-one seems to know what has happened. What do you think has happened Dad?"

"I don't know for sure son, but I think your mother and brothers may have been right, and I thought they were the crazy ones!" This thing this sequence of events isn't just happening in Israel - it's happening all over the world. Millions of people have disappeared in a puff of smoke. One second they were there the next they were gone. I don't know where they have gone to. I just can't think straight right now" Trying to alleviate the depressing situation a bit Josh suggested a cup of coffee. "I will make us both a mug of steaming hot coffee. It won't provide the answers but maybe it will help us think better"

"Let me make the coffee dad, I need to do something"

Josh watched his son walk disconsolately towards the kitchen. He let his eyes wander around the room and as he did so, he caught sight of a book lying on the table, one book in particular that Ruth had been reading. Ruth had been reading a great deal lately. She had also bought rather large note-pads and had been writing reams of notes with charts and all sorts of weird stuff. He walked over to the table and picked the book up. Thoughtfully he ran his fingers over the words on the cover, 'Holy Bible' He casually flicked through the pages, as he did so he noticed certain words underlined in different coloured marker pens. There were notes in the margins, no mistaking Ruth's neat handwriting. She had written notes on many pages of the book, 'Wonder why she did that' thought Josh. Ruth never writes on books. Realization began to dawn on Josh. He turned to the back of the book noticing numerous hand-written notes. As he read some of the notes he suddenly realized that the book probably held some clues as to what exactly had hit their world, this new reality that they were living in right now. 'Perhaps this book will tell me what has happened and where she has gone' thought Josh to himself.

Joel returned with two steaming mugs of hot coffee only to find his father immersed in this book he had just picked up - a book of all things, at a time like this. 'The whole world has gone crazy and my dad picks up....A book.'

"Dad how can you read at a time like this ......surely you can do something a bit more positive than that"

"This isn't just any book Joel it's your mom's scripture book: Her Bible. Look she has written clear notes on the back cover listing all the things that are going to happen. She describes some of the things that are happening right now. She even mentions this disappearance of millions of people, RAPTURE she calls it. She has made this note, Thessalonians 5v3 'The day of The Lord will come unexpectedly like a thief in the night' she also wrote. 'That day will not come until two things happen, first there will be a rebellion against God and then the man of Lawlessness is revealed. He will sit in the Temple of God proclaiming that he himself is God. That is in 2nd Thessalonians ch. 2v3. Here look see for yourself' Josh handed the book to his son to read.

Joel read over some of the paragraphs. "Uh-huh! So what does all this stuff mean exactly? I can't make any sense of it. What is this 'Rapture" thing?" responded Joel with disgust promptly handing the book back to Josh.

"I had forgotten you didn't manage along to David's welcome

home dinner until later. It was David who produced a chart explaining this Rapture event as being a period of time when all the believers in Jesus would suddenly disappear from the face of the earth and be caught up into Heaven. Ben Solomon tried to explain all this to me and like you I thought he was talking nonsense. It all sounded so far-fetched at the time, and I had other things on my mind then. Sit down and I will try to explain what I can remember, not that I know a great deal more than you but the answers are in there somewhere. We just have to find out from this book what happens next!"

For the next few hours both men read their own Hebrew scriptures more diligently than they had ever done before. Ruth's notes proved most helpful. It appeared to Josh that Ruth had known the men in her life would need to know what was going to happen when they discovered the real truth and the real reason why millions of people had suddenly disappeared from the face of the earth.

" Good grief!" exclaimed Josh. "Look at this. Your Mother would have been in her element with all of this. She loved her Maths" He read aloud from 'The Book of Daniel chapter 9 v 24-27'

'Someday a decree will be made to rebuild the walls of Jerusalem, sixty nine prophetic 'weeks' after that decree, the Messiah would make His first coming. A prophetic week has always meant seven Hebrew years consisting of 360 days per year. Joel continued. 'So that means 69 weeks would be:-

69 (Weeks/years) multiplied by 7(days) = 483 years x360 (Hebrew year = 173,880 days.

The decree of Artaxerxes to rebuild the temple is recorded in the Book of Nehemiah chapter 2v1

Mum has written here 14th May 445 BC.That means before Christ doesn't it?' queried Joel. She has written here in brackets the Jewish year 4205'

'Yes.....BC stands for BEFORE CHRIST in the gentile calendar anyway' replied Josh. "Go on..... what else does it say?"

Joel continued, "Mum has also written:

173,880 days divided by 365 DAYS TO GIVE YEARS

Add that sum to the date 445BC the answer works out at 6th April AD 32 The day YESHUA/ Jesus made His entry into Jerusalem riding on a donkey!

"She then refers to the book of Daniel where it says 'HE would be cut off'

Mom has written crucified next to 'cut off'. She also cross references it to the Gospel of John chapter 12v14 which describes the actual entry of YESHUA into Jerusalem....'

Joel and Josh looked at each other in astonishment.

'This is one of Daniels prophesies fulfilled TO THE DAY' muttered Josh. 'Who would believe that? According to this YESHUA is the Messiah.

'Why couldn't our Rabbis check the math as these Christians have done? You can bet your mother would have checked this out with a fine tooth comb'. Perhaps we wouldn't be in this mess today.

"Mum did try to tell us dad... but we simply wouldn't listen"

"I know" replied Josh wearily. "What else has she written?"

More scripture verses, this time from Jeremiah chapter 25v11

"The whole land shall be desolate, and an atonement. And these nations shall serve the King of Babylon for 70 years."

'Mum then writes that Cyrus of Persia (Iran today) conquered Babylon in 536BC Cyrus even paid to allow the Jews held in captivity to return to Jerusalem to rebuild the second temple under Nehemiah.

Our own scriptures are stating to the day that these events happened. We can't make them up or change history to suit our personal viewpoint. These facts did happen away back then nearly 3,000 years ago. Who would believe all of this except we are living in those days, now as we speak" "What else does her book say?"

"More verses" replied Joel from Ezekiel this time chapter 4v3—6

God told Ezekiel to write the following:-

'A sign to the House of Israel:

Lie on your LEFT side, and bear the iniquity of the House of Israel for 390 days. Then lie on your right side and bear the iniquity of the house of Judah 40 days. I HAVE APPOINTED YOU A YEAR FOR A DAY.

Using the year for a day principle, the total 390+40 days would be equal to 430 years, the number of years Israel spent in exile from the land, for her sins. The next verse from Leviticus chapter 26v18 reads:

'IF YOU STILL DISOBEY ME I will punish you seven times more severely for your sins. Mum goes on:

430 years (lying on side) subtract 70 years of warning = 360 years

360 years multiply by 7 as Moses instructed.=2520 days

2520 days multiplied by 360 days in a Jewish year = 907,200 days

907,200 days divided by 365 days in a lunar year =2485.47

2485.47 years subtract 536 years since Cyrus decree=1949.47

Allow deductions for leap years and the fact that the Jewish year commences in April. The answer works out to......

14th MAY 1948 - Both Joel and Josh looked at each other in astonishment.

THE VERY DAY ISRAEL BECAME A NATION.

Josh made a grab for the notes "let me see those notes, I don't believe this' Josh grabbed his calculator at the same time. Made the rapid calculation and the date came out exactly the same:

The year to the exact date that Israel became an independent nation

"How can this be" said Josh "these words and dates were penned more than three and a half thousand years ago" Both men were shell shocked at these revelations.

"They all come from the Jewish scriptures not the Christian scriptures" commented Joel. "No one told us, now it is too late. We are left behind"

"They tried to tell us Joel. Just like our ancestors we were too proud too stubborn to listen. We can't blame anyone else except ourselves. Does it tell us what happens next? Do we really want to know? I do remember David getting excited and nattering on about the tribulation that follows the RAPTURE. Has your mum got any notes to follow these revelations?"

Joel randomly flicked through the pages of his mom's Bible. One passage caught his attention it was coloured differently with a marker pen.'GOD SO LOVED THE WORLD THAT HE SENT HIS ONLY SON. THAT WHOSOEVER BELIEVES IN HIM SHOULD NOT PERISH BUT HAVE EVERLASTING LIFE'

Well your Mum Gershom David and all the other messianic Jewish believers and Christians believed those words. We paid no heed I suggest we don't make the same idiotic mistake a second time. We had better read and learn all we can about the things to come. This time we will be better prepared.

"What are we going to do dad?" its total mayhem and chaos out there. What about food, we will need some provisions. What about our power source, we need power for TV our phones, computers. Roads are impassible right now. I should really go to the hospital and see if I can help with the casualties that must be filling our accident and emergency departments. My head just can't compute all of this right now"

"I don't know what we can do. First of all when it is a bit quieter I think we should move down to the Mossad safe town house in Hamalka Street. It has its own power source, and also food, well tins of food anyway. We can pick up some fresh produce in YEHUDA MAHANE market so at least we won't starve not for a few weeks anyway. It has a large comfortable underground apartment. That was where our leaders vacated to while the bombs and bullets were firing in the battle for Jerusalem. The Jewish leaders directed the war from this flat. Remember we won that war and have won every other war we have engaged in since that time. This seems to be the war we must win hands down. We are in a situation no one on earth has ever encountered before however we seem to have a God who hasn't totally abandoned the peoples of earth. HE warned us this was going to happen so hopefully your mum will have written notes so we will find clues to what is going to happen next. I'm not too hot on conspiracy theories however directing weapons and strategies during a time of war is very much within my remit"

"I keep expecting mum to walk in the front door and dump a bag of groceries in the kitchen as usual. I just can't believe they are gone, and not coming back"

"It is true what they say Joel we don't appreciate people until one day they are no longer with us. Wonder how many people are like us, reading their mum, friends and family Bible's, bet there are many in every country on the planet. Husbands like me who thought their wives were religious fanatics talking nonsense"

"This stuff scares me rigid" commented Joel. "Listen to this. Under the headingTRIBULATION SIGNS

Chapter 29

TRIBULATION SIGNS

There is going to be death, famines, floods, hurricanes, earthquakes, plagues, and epidemics, on such a scale that the earth has never seen before. This verse in Zechariah chapter 14v12 reads:

"The Lord will send a plague on all those who fought Jerusalem. They will become like walking corpses, their flesh rotting away, their eyes will shrivel in their sockets, and their tongues will decay in their mouths'

'That could accurately describe a nuclear fall-out' responded Josh.

'So can the verses in the Ezekiel war, chapter 37, 38 and 39. Looks like we had better study this in detail Listen to this. They will take 7 months to bury the dead. Whenever they find a human bone they must not touch it. They will set up a marker to it. Millions of people will die. That is after the Gog Magog war. That must absolutely be nuclear fallout after a nuclear detonation. It would release tons of black carbon blocking out the sun's rays. That in turn would cause the earth's temperature to drop causing a kinetic effect on weather patterns, which would lead to a nuclear winter. Acid rain would then destroy crops trees vegetation livestock fresh water sources would be contaminated. Food would also be contaminated, famine would soon follow.

'You forgot to mention the damage from bio terrorist chemical warfare missiles that would be unleashed at the same time. Heaven only knows what kind of viruses and epidemics we will be dealing with then. Oh man ever wished you had listened to your Mother, they warned us about all this. Ben Solomon warned me personally all this was going to happen. I dismissed it all and went to work. My head can't cope with any more study for the moment. Let's try to sleep for a few hours then we can work on a plan of action later. I will try and contact my team at HQ. They will have less an idea what is going on than we do"

"Do you think they will believe you any more than we believed Mum Gershom or David?"

"Maybe not" answered Josh. "But millions of people over the planet have disappeared in the twinkling of an eye. They must have all gone somewhere. This is the only explanation that makes any kind of sense"

I have to try and make them listen and believe. We have to prepare for the next wave that is coming. Lifting Ruth's Bible and her notes. Josh said, with all this evidence they will have to go some to come up with a better theory. I will also stop in and pick up notes and books from Ben and Julia's place. We can gather supplies on the way to the townhouse"

****

After a few hours fitful sleep Josh and Joel wakened to some coffee and NEWS. At least the power had switched back on. However it was all rather depressing to. It was utter chaos and no one had a clue as to what had just happened or indeed what was happening. Plenty daft theories flying around, the best was abduction by aliens to another planet somewhere. Thankfully Hamalka Street was not too far from The Jaffa Gate. They would have to walk as transport had been abandoned shops were open but no shop staff in the shops. Joel and Josh entered the supermarket picked up as much produce as they could carry. No point in attempting to pay as Ben Solomon's words came back to haunt Josh. 'No one would be able to buy or sell without the mark of the beast' His heart chilled at the thought of what was going to happen in the future. He shook his head no time to dwell on that right now. Work and work fast gather food supplies, pull his team together then get to work on strategy. If Ruth's notes were correct and Josh had no doubt what so ever they were, then this coming conflict was going to be the war to end all wars. Josh no longer doubted the truth of the Bible, both old and new testaments. He also realized all of the action would center round Israel. 'Almighty God, help us' prayed Josh fervently.

Josh and Joel managed to pick up a large supply of food as much as they could carry. Then they made their way to the town house. Only Josh had keys and this place was protected more securely than fort Knox there was very little chance of looting or anyone troubling them there. Josh had taken a few family heirlooms from home that reminded him of Ruth. He had wandered into David's room noting his clothes computer games CD music discs his mobile phone. It was quiet, deathly quiet. No sound of human voices. The room was empty just like Josh's life. Most of his family had gone how he wished he could have gone with them. Josh sighed, a deep weary sigh then quietly closed the door. Josh had also lifted some of Ruth's books and her note-book's. She always had been a copious note-taker.

He could not face them at the moment but he knew he would be extremely grateful for the information contained in them to make some sense of the craziness they were all living in at this time. No wonder Ruth had underlined on the front cover of one of her notebooks 'LUKE chapter 21v26 'and men's hearts will faint with fear at this time.'

****

The men settled into their new home very quickly. It was very quiet, safe, and now well stocked. They would be comfortable there for quite a while yet. Much would depend on the next sequence of events.

Joel cycled to Hadassah hospital the following morning with great trepidation wondering what on earth he would encounter. He too like Josh had very quickly come to believe in God and YESHUA time to learn to pray.

Josh was very pleasantly surprised to find out his team were around and happy to come to the townhouse to meet up. Andrew Gordon and Fitz came along with Judy. The mood of the team was quiet and somber. There was none of the usual banter that normally went on within the team.

Josh sat at his desk and looked carefully at each member of his team. They looked to him for leadership. He noted the confusion, the unposed questions each one wanted to ask. It was time to speak; he wanted to share with his team what he knew. However it was Judy direct as usual, who started the ball rolling.

"Josh we don't know what on earth is going on here, we have

plenty of questions, zero answers. If you have any idea can you share what has just happened with us please?"

"Yes….. I know" sighed Josh. "I'm pretty certain I know what has happened. You are going to find this difficult to believe, so grab a chair and I will fill you in as best I can on this strange phenomenon"

"I suppose phenomenon is as good a word as any to describe what has happened. Have we been invaded by aliens or something even more sinister" ventured Micah seriously.

"No, not exactly aliens, unless you consider the Messiah to be an alien" replied Josh.

"THE MESSIAH" chorused the team in unison.

"Josh, be serious. This is no time for jokes" replied Micah irritably. "This whole situation is far too serious to kid around with. This is not funny"

"I am being perfectly serious Micah. My whole family apart from Joel and I, have disappeared, vanished literally off the face of the earth. Have any of you guys lost any family members or friends?"

"Only one of the team answered yes to that question. Ari's little sister had disappeared. Ari said she used to meet on the beach with a huge crowd of young folks in the Galilee area. They danced and sang lived almost communally with each other and called themselves messianic believers. Ari said his parents believed this was a phase she would grow out of but now she too had disappeared"

Then Judy said thoughtfully. "Has no-one else noticed all the kids have gone? Not one child under bar mitzvah age has been left. Every single child has vanished. No one seems to have any idea where the children have been taken. The only thing we hear is Rachel weeping for her children"

Gordon spoke quietly. "I think I know what you are leading up to Josh." everyone turned to Gordon in surprise. He was very well respected by every member of the Mossad, especially those he had worked with. They knew him to be highly intelligent, resourceful honest with a wealth of knowledge and information on subjects they knew very little about. In fact it was all above their pay grade, highly secretive secret service stuff. He spoke seven languages fluently, was extremely well travelled and had worked in Bletchley Park as one of their code breakers. When Gordon spoke people listened. They listened now.

Gordon turned to Josh and asked. "Do you remember just before the missile attack I told you my father was an avid Zionist" "yes I recall that, we didn't get much further in our conversation, events rather took over. I didn't understand then I think I do now. Has your father disappeared and your mother too?"

Gordon nodded. "Exactly, do I tell them or do you?"

"You tell them. I presume you know more about this whole thing than I do. I'm still coming to terms with the whole issue. Still hoping and praying this is my worst nightmare and I will waken up to find it was all a bad dream"

"We really don't mind who tells us as long as someone does. What is going on? What is the big secret?" urged Judy impatiently. "We just need one of you to tell us we don't actually mind who"

Gordon cleared his throat. "My father was a country Vicar similar to one of your Rabbi's. I grew up to be a Preachers kid, but I didn't inherit my father's faith. As a youngster I had to attend church and listen to hundreds of boring sermons. I suppose I heard the truth but in my eyes church was for old people and wee kids. I was into science, and code breaking was my first love. I didn't realize until too late, Jesus or your YESHUA isn't into religion either. He is into relationship. I was a stupid boy who chose to listen to men instead of God.

My Father often preached that Jesus was coming back He was coming for His own. Those who chose to follow Him and have a relationship with Him. The word 'Rapture' derives from a Latin word 'RAPT' which roughly translated means to be transported from one place to another. The Apostle Paul used the Greek word HARPAZO to explain what would happen to the church in the latter days. Both words mean exactly the same. It simply means that millions of believers in Jesus will be taken from the earth into Heaven literally in the twinkling of an eye. Exactly as we have witnessed.

RAPTURE: You can read the account in the scriptures

1st THESSALONIANS chapter 4 v16.

Much like God snatched Enoch Elijah Moses Paul and John up to Heaven to be with HIM. They all describe what Heaven was like for us

So the Rapture that I did not believe would happen has in fact happened"

That statement caused some unrest within the room.'

"What on earth are you talking about Gordon? I've never heard of any of this before. Are you telling us this disappearance of millions of people is this 'Rapture phenomenon?" Asked Judy totally puzzled.

"I am indeed" said Gordon.

"I happen to agree totally with what Gordon is saying" interrupted Josh."Once you have looked at the evidence and studied the information we have you will also agree with the conclusion that we have come to.

The issue we have now is where do we go from here?Every country on the planet has been affected by this…. call it phenomenon if you like. I prefer Rapture because that is what happened to my family and millions of others.

The more pressing issue is what do we do now with the information we have?Secondly do you want to know what happens next on the agenda? The choice is yours" said Josh. "The only other comment I would make is…..I have lost a beloved wife and two sons. Many close friends I cared for and respected. Meara the young lady who left her family and her village to get David and Joseph back to their families. We swapped a couple of very bad guys back to their family village in exchange for Joseph. But we chipped them first"

Gordon guffawed at that statement. "Are you saying what I think you are saying?"

"I am. I've been doing a lot of homework into this 'Deep state' shower you were talking about. Time for us to deal with them" stated Josh firmly. As Josh turned to his team he shared the best bit of news first. "Before we begin this intensive study, perhaps we should let you in on a little secret we know, that no one else does.........drum roll.... Are you ready for this?"

"Just get on with it" they all shouted at their chief. OK the best bit. All of these people who vanished in a second in the twinkling of an eye the good book explain to us in graphic detail they are coming back to earth in 7 years-time exactly'

"Josh, this all gets weirder and weirder will you please stop talking in riddles and just explain to us simply what this is all about" said Judy speaking up for all of the team.

"I will explain Judy, with Gordon's help. This is first of all top secret. You must not breathe a word of this outside of this room. It is going to be very dangerous. In fact you have no idea just how dangerous this assignment is going to become. If you think this is confusing, weird, strange, bewildering then hold on to your hats. You have experienced nothing yet. This 'Deep state' will stop at nothing to achieve total world- wide domination of every tongue, every tribe and every nation. The people who did know what was going on were The Judeo-Christian community of believers, however as you know they are no longer with us. The Holy Spirit has also been taken out of the picture therefore that allows the antichrist, the false prophet and the Islamic Mehdi to come through. As you know he is the twelfth Imam.

There is going to be a fair bit of study to go along with this assignment. You need to know who we are up against, their background, their agenda how they operate, how to recognize them. What they are going to do here in Israel, primarily in Jerusalem the prize as always is....The Third Temple on Temple Mount. I am giving you a choice if you want to be a part of this team and if you want to continue with this assignment. I would also suggest that you stay here on site. It's a big chateau three stories high so plenty of free room and board. Very soon you are going to be forced to take a MARK, it will be a MICRO-CHIP placed in your head or right hand. Do not on any account take this mark I will explain why later. However that also means you become incommunicado in our safe house for everyone's safety. You will again understand why when you have all the information.

That is a brief outline. Before I go any further is there anyone who would like to leave for another assignment? Believe me there are plenty going on right now?"

The conversation and questions came fast and furious, but the important thing was, no one left. They all stayed and wanted to remain the 'A' team. They knew they were the best and Josh knew he had the best, he chose them after all. "Ok guys lets break for lunch. Gordon and I can compare notes and get them photocopied for you then Gordon can briefly give the first outline and explanation why this is all happening.First of all Gordon will explain why he Fitz Bannerman and Andrew came to Israel to warn us about this cartel operating world-wide. Our Mossad we do not believe as yet has been infiltrated. You guys have been chosen by me because I trust you, however the choice is yours. Feel free to leave if you would rather not take on this assignment"

"Well chief, that is the second time you have asked me if I

would like to take up an assignment. How can I possibly say no!! I want to know about all of this. It's way much too interesting for me to leave now"

The rest of the team felt the same. They trusted Josh they were a team. As the 'Amigos' said 'one for all and all for one'

"That is great I appreciate your loyalty and support. Time for lunch then we can get down to some serious work"

Chapter 30

The team had a whole sheaf of photo copied notes to study.

Josh explained the Tribulation period would last for 7 years. This period was very specific with clear signs and time scale: After the Rapture, signs of the times, the tribulation Gog/Magog war including the mark of the beast and the antichrist make their appearance.

Gordon shared with the team. Their adversary was the 'DEEP STATE' AIM: Total world domination: their strategies: plans and purpose.

ONE WORLD GOVERNMENT, THE CHIP, THE MARK OF THE BEAST, without it no one could buy or sell anything anywhere to anyone.

It is fair to say the team were all rather shell shocked at the end of the session.

"Do you have a plan Josh?"

"I have a basic plan. First one..... we cannot stay here long term. They have ways and means of tracking everyone and everything. They have the latest up to date technology and the brightest brains. However we do have three and a half years before the real horror story begins. In this amazing book full of information we have accurate time lines to work with.

1) We move base fairly soon down to the tunnels running under the Temple Mount. Jews since time began have hidden in these tunnels to escape their enemies. It is like a rabbit warren down there but we have the blueprint. It is not written down anywhere of course, but every first male member of the KOHANIM tribe has knowledge of the tunnel passageways. The information is always passed from father to first son.

2) I have a very good friend who has this knowledge. I absolutely trust him. When he has the verifiable knowledge that we have he will come and join us.

3) We will leave a very large food stock in many different locations all the way to the Hill of KOHLITT. There are at least sixty different locations where the Temple treasures have been hidden since Jeremiahs time. Yes, I do believe the Arc of the Covenant is located there again we have pretty strong verifiable proof from believe it or not a Christian believer's outer space scan explorer. This can be as far as 40 miles. We need to collect as much produce as we can and store safely. We need underground cable sources of high tech power. That should give us heat light and power for our technical devices. That shouldn't be too difficult for our high tech guys to arrange. We need teams down there to dig deep and lay pipes. We require huge freezers to keep the stores of food fresh for a few years if need be. Good luck to foreign invaders trying to locate us all down there.

4) Vitally important we have a fresh water source that runs all the way down from the Temple Mount - excavations

are going on as we speak. Archaeologists really don't like to be interrupted when then have cracked through to their most important finds for more than 3000 years. (They found HEZEKIAHS tunnel and a treasure trove) They are not going to be stopped now. The water source is of lifesaving importance as the water in most countries will be contaminated with nuclear waste. Yes people...... we will be facing nuclear war. Again our scriptures tell us in Ezekiel chap 38 and 39 we will be burying our dead for 7 months. We must not touch the bones or any bodies. They are marked and incinerated later.

5)   Weapons of course. Every innovative protective and offensiveweapon we have in our arsenal. Medication. Mountains of it. We must be prepared for any and every eventuality known and unknown in our battles this far.

6)   I would like you to divide into small groups and let's thrash this out. We need to have a clear time line for the different challenges that will come one after the other. They are all written down clearly for each person to memorize. We have a better chance of surviving than most because we have the handbook here with the survival strategies.

✳✳✳✳✳✳✳✳✳✳✳✳✳✳✳✳✳✳✳✳✳✳✳✳✳✳✳✳✳✳✳

There was very little discussion as the team perused Ruth's copied notes. It was Micah who passed comment first. "Goodness these are our scriptures from our TANAKH our TORAH. These notes cover virtually every book in our Torah are they all talking about this Jesus being our Messiah? Then she compares notes in all the Christian scriptures. They are saying almost exactly the same thing. Ruth must have spent hours and hours in study. Certainly fascinating but what has it got to do with our present situation?"

"Quite a lot as it happens! this is the key to everything we are facing right now. We are living the last few chapters of our age - they are being played out as we speak. Let me explain" replied Gordon.

"According to the last book in Christian scriptures called 'The book of Revelation' everything is revealed ahead of time. We have an advantage over most of the people still alive at this time as we have a timescale and prior warning as to what is going to happen next. We can influence some of the events and in turn warn as many people as we can. YESHUA is returning to Israel in 7 years-time at the head of a mighty army. There will be a final last conflict at Armageddon Tel Megiddo in the JEZREEL valley not far from Nazareth where Jesus was born. This valley is also where Gideon chased the Midianites with only 300 warriors. Maybe the good Lord is trying to tell us something here. We are not 300 in number but hey God plus one is a majority right?" "Right" said the team in unison. "I am also reminded of the passage where Elisha and his servant GEHAZI were staying in the city of Dothan and surrounded on all sides by the Syrian army. GEHAZI was scared understandably but Elisha prayed to God and asked Him to open his eyes to see the many hoard's of WARRIER ANGELS protecting them. God is saying to us today we do not stand alone in this battle. There are legions of angels protecting us and fighting on our behalf. Remember Archangel Michael? He watches over Israel day and night. In Daniel when the angel PALMONI was struggling against the powers and principalities. Archangel Michael came to battle on his behalf. They chased the powers and principalities back to where they came from. Our battle is not against people - always remember the demons behind the people"

"This all sounds a bit far-fetched like something out of an Indiana Jones film or something" was the wry comment from Daniel.

"Believe me Daniel it is much deadlier than that. When you read over Revelation tonight that is your night time reading by the way. You will read about the war in Heaven and what happens from there."

"Look at this note from Ruth" interrupted Judy. It's about the nuclear reactor at CHERNOBLE in the 1980s. Ruth has written the following....

REVELATION 8v10 ....'and the third angel sounded, and there fell a great star from heaven, burning as it were a lamp, and it fell upon the third part of the rivers and upon the fountains of waters, and the name of the star is wormwood and the third part of the waters became wormwood and many men died of the waters, because they were made bitter.....' end quote.

Josh added "In case anyone is wondering, wormwood is a bitter herb used in rural Russia. What is interesting to note that the UKRANIAN word for wormwood is.......CHERNOBLE......is this mere coincidence I ask you."

"What about the second part of the quote Josh? This is from Isaiah chapter 11. It speaks of the troubles that Israel will experience when the Jews return to their own land"

'He shall set up a flag for the nations and shall assemble the outcasts of Israel and gather them together the dispersed of Judah from the four corners of the earth......v 12 one of two flags shall be for nations'....... End of quote. Our people have been returning from the four corners of the earth for many years now. We have only been in our land for 100 years one generation and Jerusalem has been under our control for only 50 years. This is our flag, the symbol of Israel, the root of Jesse the Star of David. How can this all of this be mere coincidence?"

Suddenly without warning, the office shook violently followed by a loud rumble. "What in"....... exclaimed Josh jumping from his seat and moving towards the window. The entire team gathered round him listening as the rumble grew steadily louder as it drew ever nearer. Before long the entire building was shaking. Pictures fell from the wall. Machines tumbled to the floor with a crash adding to the fearsome din. A coffee machine toppled spilling its contents over the floor. The entire room seemed to be moving: tables, chairs, and desks seemed to overturn of their own accord. People were sliding and tumbling to the ground.

"What is it, what's happening?"' yelled Judy in panic.

"It's an earthquake!! Yelled Reuben pale with fear, the noise increased as the tremor moved closer. Buildings began to collapse all around them. People were being thrown around like rag dolls. Andrew tried to shield Judy with his body but she was wrenched from his grasp and went crashing against a wall where she lay motionless. Andrew stretched out to reach her as another shock wave hit the building, throwing him against the opposite wall and winding him.

Fluorescent light fittings fell from the ceiling, some of the heavy double glazed window units broke free and fell crashing onto the street below. One window fell into the room and hit Micah killing him instantly. Chaos and confusion abounded. Panic stricken people were shouting and screaming, but their voiced could not be heard above the cacophony of sound engulfing them. People ran like lemmings blindly following each other in an effort to escape the pending devastation but there was no escape. In many places the ground simply tore apart and opened up revealing gaping caverns - people vehicles and even buildings disappeared into the abyss. The ruptured ground caused water and gas mains to fracture and the atmosphere quickly became heavy with the smell of gas. Electric power cables severed igniting pockets of escaping gas. Numerous fires were erupting all over the area. With the water supply ruptured fire-fighting would become difficult, if not impossible.

Chapter 31

As suddenly as they began the earth tremors stopped. The whole episode lasted less than three minutes. Survivors stood or lay where they were in complete shock. Many people were injured with blood streaming from wounds but at least they were alive. Josh and Daniel lay unconscious, covered in blood from flying glass. Andrew got slowly to his feet and moved towards Judy who was lying prostrate and not moving. Thankfully, she was still breathing. Gordon got up slowly. 'Nothing broken' he thought as he stretched his limbs slowly. He moved towards Micah who was lying trapped under the window unit and checked for signs of life. It was obvious he was dead - the huge window had fallen on him severing his throat. Gordon covered Micah's face as best he could with a jacket. The team slowly began to recover.

'Dear God' thought Gordon 'where will this all end?' The knowledge he had recently acquired suggested that what was happening now would be the very beginning of what the scriptures called 'the beginning of sorrows'. The most horrendous period of human history had begun and was about to become a million times worse. This must be 'the time of Jacob's trouble' as Jeremiah stated in Jeremiah 30 v7 a time of tribulation such as mankind had never before witnessed. He also remembered the words of Jesus as recorded in Matthew 24v22 which offered him a modicum of comfort. Jesus said,

'He would cut short the tribulation short for the sake of HIS elect otherwise no human being would survive the onslaught of the evil one.'

'Josh groaned and struggled to move his numbed body into action. Gordon turned his attention to him. "Can you tell me where you are hurt? I can't see blood anywhere. Let me check for broken bones or other injuries""I'm fine" assured Josh. Render first aid to the injured then organize the team........' Josh managed to struggle onto a chair and Daniel righted an upturned table. "Gather round" said Josh. "Those in need of first aid get patched up. The rest of us will help as much as we can, but stay in pairs. Michael Daniel will you get poor Micah out of here please. I will try and contact Hadassah hospital I want to see how Joel is and to see if we can help anywhere. Let's report back here in an hour"

The line to Hadassah was dead. Gordon tried his mobile; it too was dead. When Josh looked out of the window all he could see was the utter devastation everywhere: destroyed buildings and numerous fires raging. This building was a Mossad safe house and so largely protected to some degree.

As Josh surveyed the scene he remembered a couple of Julia Solomon's notes that he had found amongst Ruth's belongings. From the book of Zechariah he had just read last night before retiring to bed..........Zechariah 14v3-8

'and on that day. HIS feet will stand on the Mount of Olives which will be split apart in two making a wide valley running east to west. The notes also explained that the movement of the Tectonic plates boundary separating the Arabian and African geological plates would cause the Dead Sea to join with the

Mediterranean Sea. The earthquake they had just experienced was simply another sign that they were indeed living in the latter days.'

"How many lives have been lost this day" Josh wondered: "how much more can our small nation endure. Hundreds if not thousands of lives must have been lost" He prayed his son would still be alive and helping to save many more lives in Hadassah. He tried to contact Joel one more time but the power was still down.

It was several weeks before the true extent of the earthquake damage became clear. The clean-up operation took months. Virtually every family in the country had lost loved ones, many with little hope of recovering the bodies for decent burial. There had been some miracles too - rescue teams had managed to save many people from certain death against all odds. Thanks to the swift and well co - ordinated action by the Israeli department of health the spread of disease that normally accompanies such disasters was virtually eliminated.

Perhaps one of the greatest shocks that stunned everyone living in Jerusalem both Israeli and Arab alike was the total destruction of the Dome of the Rock. HARAM AL SHARIF that had stood atop the Temple Mount for more than1300 years. The Mosque was an impressive symmetrical, octagonal structure. The exterior was covered in azure blue tiles whilst the building itself was topped with a gleaming bronze dome that shone like gold. The Mosque stood in what was considered to be the most important spot in all Jerusalem. It was the third most holy shrine in the world of Islam even though Mohammad himself had never set foot in Jerusalem, nor is Jerusalem mentioned in the Koran. Muslim tradition states that Mohammad was carried to Jerusalem on al-burak a winged horse which had the face of a woman and the tail of a peacock. The Mosque was now reduced to rubble after the earthquake, yet the Western Wall sacred to the Jews and situated only meters away stood intact.

He knew that legends and historical facts are totally irrelevant where people's religion was concerned but the destruction of the mosque weighed heavily on Josh all that day. He was fearful as to what the following days would bring. Despite the obvious suffering of the people and the Dome of the Rock Mosque being destroyed, would result in serious unrest so trouble would undoubtedly lie ahead, of that he was fairly certain.

The Arab population publicly mourned for their destroyed Holy site and most of the Jewish population understood the depth of feeling involved. Throughout Jerusalem an amazing cooperation took place as both Arab and Jew worked together side by side trying to rebuild what was left of their city. Perhaps it would only be a short time before the simmering resentments of hundreds of years of feuding reared its ugly head once again.

Chapter 32

Many parts of mainland Europe had also been affected by the violent earthquakes although not to the same extent as Jerusalem. Across the Atlantic in the United States of America, millions of citizens had also vanished during the same period as those in other parts of the world. The Mid-West the traditional 'Bible belt' experienced the greatest number of people disappearing. Similar reports were received from the four corners of the world.

Western Europe had not suffered the same loss of life, thus allowing vital rescue services to be resumed relatively quickly. Within five days of the quake, heads and representatives of State were summoned to Rome for an emergency crisis meeting. The conference was referred to by those attending as a 'Club of Rome' The meeting was stormy and contentious to say the least with emotions running high. In attendance at the meeting was a dark haired handsome young man, with unusually clear blue eyes. He listened intently to every debate, to the hysterical demands and detected the real underlying fear in the voices of those who spoke. After a short period he moved to the floor of the auditorium and took up position at the Presidents table. His action caused the assembly to focus their attention on him. Almost at once the noise faded away. This man's bearing was tall and erect with a commanding presence. Power seemed to emanate from him. He was dressed in a finely tailored grey suit and expensive soft leather shoes. His appearance was immaculate and perfectly coordinated in every aspect. His very presence dominated the conference hall without any apparent effort on his part. Every eye turned to look and to listen to what this man had to say.

He was very relaxed, a natural orator who spoke easily using humour effectively. He surprised the leaders of the different nations by addressing them fluently in their own language. He surprised them further by having an amazing knowledge and understanding of the problems facing each country represented.

Seated in the conference hall was Sir Malcolm Ewing, the Cabinet Minister and British representative to the Council. Beside him on his left was the American Vice President Peter Andrews. Sir Malcolm whispered to the American "who is this fellow?"

"The new boy wonder......Maurice LEVIAN" replied Andrews. "I believe he is an economist. A bit of political strategist..... He is from Switzerland originally half Jewish but he keeps that part very quiet....firmly declares he is non-religious."

The American pointed across the room "LEVIAN is the protégé of Alfredo Marks the Etruscan sitting over there second row to the right"

"Ah yes I see him" replied Sir Malcolm. "Where did you gather all this information from?"

"One of our guys.... Jim Bannerman, he has been compiling information on this guy for some time. He filled me in on a 'need to know' basis a few months ago. Bannerman was convinced that some world-wide conspiracy was being organized. Quite interesting I must say what he has managed to uncover" Andrews continued, "The Mossad in Israel provided us with the information that led us to the Etruscan connection" Motioning across the room, "we think Marks is the brains behind the operation.... As yet we haven't managed to come up with any conclusive evidence..... He keeps a very low profile, taking great care to cover any involvement he may have"

"Are the Jews briefed on the details?"

"No not yet. They are still not in communication with us or with you British for that matter. They think our governments have sold them out to the Arabs.Can't say I blame them it certainly looks that way. Bannerman was furious when he discovered what both our governments had been up to. It didn't help when Gus MacGregor our envoy assigned to organize the Middle East Peace talks vanished off the face of the earth along with a few million other people a few months ago"

Sir Malcolm nodded, "Yes this disappearance thing was mighty strange........" Their conversation was cut short as Maurice LEVIAN moved from the floor of the auditorium and took up position on the Presidents podium where he began addressing the assembly.

"My dear colleagues" he began quietly. "Our nations have survived some very strange situations and traumas over the past few months. Many of our countries are still in turmoil, Talk of despair, and hopelessness abounds. However we the leaders of our nations must have great hope for the future. From this present disorder and confusion we have an opportunity to build a better world. We can bring order out of chaos if we work together, one with the other. Our real strength lies in a new World Government, under which we can be integrated economically, politically, and defensively. Unity is the key to future success. United we stand divided we fall. We have an opportunity now to create a New World Order......."

Delegates from each country listened as if mesmerized - they hung on every word as Maurice LEVIAN continued to outline his plans for The New World Order. "Our first priority must be to rebuild and restructure our towns and cities for our people he said. "At the same time a centrally coordinated security force will be required in every city to ensure that ordinary citizens can safely walk the streets again. Criminals will be dealt with most severely. Harsh custodial sentences will be given to those who offend against the State. I propose that electronic tagging be introduced to subversive elements; to rapists, looters and terrorists. We can and we will make our streets safe to walk again" He thundered with passion "We will build a strong One World government" Collectively we will become the new world peace keepers. Many countries represented here today produce more food and resources than they need. We will share it equally with our poorer brothers in countries that need our help. Let us work together to build a new and better world for future generations!" LEVIAN continued his passionate speech without notes for twenty minutes. At the end of his oration he was greeted with thunderous applause. Interrupting the applause, the Etruscan Alfredo Marks proposed that LEVIAN be elected to head 'The New World Order' Government. As if rehearsed the majority of leaders and delegates present arose as one applauding the suggestion. There was no need to count dissenters the odds were overwhelmingly in favour of electing Maurice LEVIAN, President of The New World Order.

Chapter 33

LEVIAN spent the next few weeks travelling the world and meeting leaders of every nation. His natural charm charisma and wisdom in political strategy easily disarmed potential enemies persuading them to become allies. He was surely the most gifted diplomat the world had ever known. Under his leadership he seemed to be able to resurrect old fashioned moral values. He actively encouraged people to attend church. On his recommendation his friend Cardinal Stravinski was elected head of the 'WORLD COUNCIL OF CHURCHES'. Together they advocated a 'ONE WORLD CHURCH' the only dissenting voices came from the Middle East.......from the Arabs and the Jews.

****

During late November whilst at their Etruscan residence, LEVIAN and Stravinski got around to discussing the Middle East question.

"How do you intend solving this problem of The Arabs and the Jews No one has ever been able to overcome that major problem as yet; It's rather a poisoned chalice I would say"

"I have given this matter some considerable thought and I have a plan. This strategy should go some way to resolving the matter"

"You do? How? I am very interested in this plan. Everyone

that has tried has so far failed. What ace do you hold up your sleeve?"

"Simple, give the Jews what they want more than anything else in the world, their Temple and a peace pact with their Arab neighbours. Once we give them that they will hail me as their saviour and fall into line with all of our plans. Believe me the Jews will present no problem" stated LEVIAN with conviction.

"uh-huh' Well I can't say I am completely convinced" responded a doubtful Stravinsky 'How are you going to deliver this package? The Arabs will not accept this proposal readily; they are still an economic power and still own two thirds of the world's oil reserves - a fair bargaining chip. The Arab nations will all unite and come against us"

"No I don't believe they will. I have already dealt with that problem. Most Arabs like money and power. We arrange one or two 'accidents' to any dissidents among them and replace them with more reasonable people who have a great desire to work with us. They are more pragmatic than religious. They realize we wield more power and expertise than they do. They also want to live and be cooperating. With us they get power over the masses, not complete power of course.....Trust me they will do exactly what I want them to do. I have already held meetings with some of our more influential Arab friends. They will deal with any extremist hotheads in their ranks. I freely admit the Jews will be more difficult however they too are pretty pragmatic they know I will take care of them providing they play ball with me and they get their Temple. They will not give us any bother if we simply leave them to it and keep the Arabs sweet elsewhere"

Cardinal Stravinski gave a low whistle of admiration. "That is pure genius Maurice. I am impressed, you never fail to amaze me with your brilliance......I truly believe this might work"

"No doubt about it of course it will work" declared a confident LEVIAN. We leave in two days-time for Israel. There we will be met by the new chief Rabbi of Jerusalem, and give him the good news he can make a start building his temple. Our 'peace keeping force' will be there to make sure that any Arabs thinking about upsetting our peace plan will be convinced very rapidly to desist. Anyone who steps out of line will disappear. Everyone will have our MARK shortly then there will be no hiding place for anyone, anywhere then"

"Well I can certainly see that taking shape rapidly. Just one question, I can't figure out why you want me to come to Israel with you?"

"Of course you must come with me. You are head of the One World Church. All churches, all religions come under the banner of the World council of churches, of which you are head. Religion is a very useful tool it is an opiate to lull the masses into a false sense of security. It suits my purposes for the moment"

LEVIAN looked at Stravinski and continued. "Money and greed are powerful allies. Thanks to the offers we have made to shareholders our corporation more or less has control of all our targeted key industries. The next step is to introduce our 'micro dot implantation programme' once everyone has had their 'CHIP' inserted we will then have complete control"

Stravinski looked into LEVIAN's cold blue eyes and shuddered. 'Pure unadulterated evil' he thought. No man could stand against

LEVIAN. He was obsessed with power. He will have power at all costs. Woe betide any person who attempts to come against him, he would dispose of them as easily as swatting a fly. Stravinski was not easily frightened but he was afraid of this man.

215

Chapter 33

JERUSALEM

Two days later Josh and the team were sitting in their headquarters watching a news programme on TV. 'So that's him' thought Josh as he observed LEVIAN shaking hands with the Chief Rabbi on Temple Mount Jerusalem. The World Leader and the Chief Rabbi were standing on the site where the Haram al Sharif the Muslim Dome of the Rock Mosque, had stood before the earthquake caused its collapse several months previously. This was a sacred site to both Jew and Arab alike. Now it had been given by The World Government on LEVIAN'S instructions to the Jews. Here they would build a new third temple on the very same spot that Abraham had tried to sacrifice his son, and later King David had intended to build a home for The Arc of the Covenant. The Jews were ecstatic that at last they had their historic sacred site firmly in their sole possession once more.

Satellite communication had recently been restored thanks to the influence of Maurice LEVIAN. Live television pictures of the laying of the foundation stone were being beamed to every nation. The sound of the shofar could be heard throughout Jerusalem. The blowing of the ram's horn was normally reserved for ushering in Shabbat and for special Holy days in the Jewish calendar such as the Day of Atonement, Yom Kippur and The Jewish New Year. Today it was being sounded to herald in a new era in Jewish history, the day that marked the laying of the foundation stone of the New Third temple. There was a carnival atmosphere not only in Jerusalem, but throughout Israel. People were dancing in the streets music playing people singing everywhere. The catastrophic earthquake of a few months ago seemed consigned to distant history. Thanks to Maurice LEVIAN there was a new air of confidence in the Middle East.

Gordon left the room to fetch drinks as Josh stood alone gazing out of the window. As he looked over the golden city, he cast his mind back to 1967 when Jerusalem had been brought back into Jewish hands after 2000 years. He recalled what Jerusalem had been like that day, much like the day Israel was granted independence in 1948 I should think. He could sense the same air of excitement today. They hailed Maurice LEVIAN like a Messiah, how long will it be before this antichrist shows his true colours. 'He truly is a wolf in sheep's clothing and has pulled the wool over millions of people's eyes' thought Josh. 'We had better make sure we are well ahead with our preparations to camp underground deep down the tunnels where LEVIAN'S troops cannot detect us'

Andrew and Judy were first to return to the safe house. He could hear them laughing with excitement as they ran up the last flight of stairs before bursting into the communal living room. The door swung open with a clatter, they were behaving like a couple of boisterous school kids - honestly! They were followed by Joel, Fitz and remaining team members.

"Hi Josh you are missing an amazing celebration down at the Western Wall tonight. It is really great fun. Why are you downcast? Do you not believe this guy can keep his promises to ISRAEL?"

"No Judy I do not trust him. I believe we are witnessing the antichrist perform right under our noses. I have studied every clue the Bible give us about this guy. Some of us have been meeting up regularly to examine and study the scriptures. It has been a complete revelation how much the New Testament is similar to our own scriptures. What came to me tonight as I watched the Celebration was Matthews Gospel Chapter 24 it says'

"That the antichrist will stand in the Holy place and desecrate the Temple, he will carry out the Abomination of Desolation that Daniel warned us about 3000 years ago in Daniel chapter 9 then on to chapters 10, 11 and 12.You young folk must understand the dangerous times we are living in right now. Construction of the new Temple will allow the antichrist to fulfill 'the Prophesy of Daniel' written down for us all these years ago. This guy fits the picture down to the last detail. Look at how quickly he has built up and organized the World defense Federation, all in the name of a strong peace keeping force. He will soon be strong enough to throw away any PRETENCE of a peaceful leader. He is a power hungry jackal. Have you noticed there never seems to be any dissenting voices anywhere?"

"I guess I haven't been paying much attention lately" confessed Judy, glancing over at Andrew. He shrugged his shoulders responding only with a cheeky grin.

'Ah ha, what a time to fall in love' thought Josh. The whole world is going to hades in a basket, it's falling apart at the seams and two of my best team members have better things to occupy their time than notice what is going on in the world around them. Only two young people in love would consider a relationship at this time. He couldn't help a wry smile to himself just the same.

However Andrew was listening he asked Josh "what dissenters?"

"Exactly!" was the loud response from Josh. There is none!" Remember these people primarily in UK and America who were nominal Sunday church goers the ones who were left behind along with us when all the born again messianic Christian and Jewish believers were Raptured" Some of the people left behind were church pastors and Ministers clergymen of various denominations the ones who only preached a social gospel leaving out the heart of Jesus teaching. What has happened to them, where are they now? Those people now know the truth. Like me they now know believing is not enough! Goodness me even the demons and antichrist believe but they tremble with fear and trembling. They now know a person must be spiritually reborn and filled with the power of the Holy Spirit. They were too late to go with Jesus the first time round but we know that He is coming back in 7 years-time and we don't intend being left behind a second time.

"I don't get your meaning Josh. Why would this guy LEVIAN eliminate ministers and church leaders he openly encourages religious attendance" replied Judy.

"He does but only on his terms. The only ministers allowed to preach openly can only do so in churches under the auspices of the World Council of churches where he has control. Those who are reported to be preaching the truth from the Holy Scriptures are very rapidly losing their heads I mean they are literally being 'beheaded' They are vanishing, being murdered and made a spectacle of for preaching the truth. The other issue of course, they are refusing to take the mark. They know the scriptures are speaking the truth so they have to speak the truth now even though they are likely to die for speaking out publicly"

"Gordon was sharing all of this with us the other day" said Andrew. "He was saying thousands of believers have to go on the run and live underground. They didn't get the time we did to prepare for such a time as this. You have prepared us for the time coming when no man will be able to eat or drink and their hearts will faint with fear. They will be frightened to the very core of their being. The only way to cope with the coming terrors is to hide under the shadow of the Almighty"

Josh said quietly but with utter conviction

"We have a myriad of secret tunnels all the way to Qumran and beyond. Good luck to anyone finding us down there if they don't know where they are going. Our problem will be if someone infiltrates our ranks and will then be in a position to betray us.

I have given considerable thought to this. I believe we keep the tunnel leading to Hill of Kohlitt very secret. Only our inner core team will have this information. We have it covered and stocked to last at least the seven years if need be. Then the Messiah returns to take HIS rightful place. We will join this end time army and see the antichrist thrown into the pit and chained up for a thousand years. However the next seven years are not for anyone fearful of heart.

THE BATTLE OF ARMAGEDDON is the battle to end all battles. YESHUA is coming back for HIS own our job is to stay alive and make sure we are not left behind a second time"

THE END FOR NOW

Pictures and Illustrations

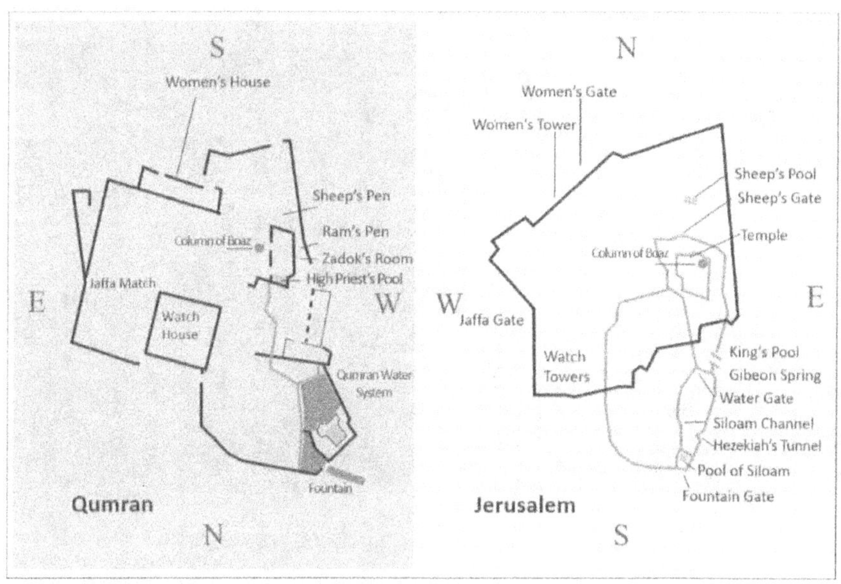

Figure 1: Qumran and Jerusalem

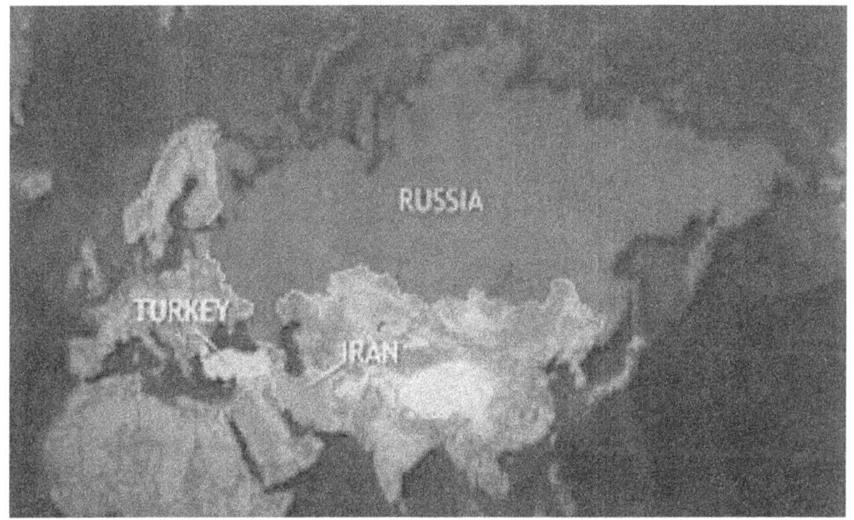

Figure 2: Russia, Turkey and Iran

Figure 3: Temple Mount, Jerusalem

Figure 4: Hezekiah's Tunnel, beneath Temple Mount, Jerusalem

Figure 5: Pool of Siloam Tunnel, beneath Temple Mount, Jerusalem

Figure 6: Kidron Valley, Jerusalem

Figure 7: Jewish Telegraph-Friday July 18, 2014

Figure 8: Rabbi Yitzak Kaduri, 108 years of age

Figure 9: Dead Sea Scrolls

Figure 10: Plague of Locusts Attacks
Islam's Holiest Mosque in Mecca

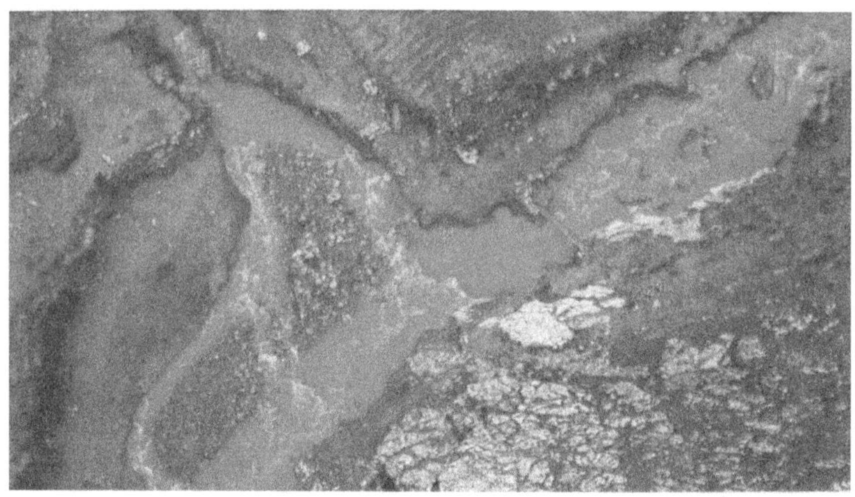

Figure 11: The Red River in Cusco Peru

Figure 12: Terhan Summit 2018: Rouhani (Iran), Erdogan (Turkey), Putin (Russia)